THROUGH THE FOG

THROUGH THE FOG

MICHAEL C. GRUMLEY

 THOMAS & MERCER

Text copyright © 2015 Michael C. Grumley
All rights reserved.

Published by Thomas&Mercer, Seattle

www.apub.com

Amazon, the Amazon logo, and Thomas&Mercer are trademarks of Amazon.com, Inc., or its affiliates.

ISBN-13: 9781477820957
ISBN-10: 1477820957

Cover design by Jason Ramirez

Library of Congress Control Number: 2014946859

Printed in the United States of America

*To my mother, who taught me humility,
gratitude, love, and how to imagine. And to
my father, who gave me the gift of dreams.*

1

He lurched upright in the darkness, his chest heaving uncontrollably. Traces of light crept in from around the window, and a much brighter glow from under the door illuminated part of his bedroom floor. The door opened a moment later, blinding him in the glare.

"Evan, are you okay?"

From his bed, he looked up at the silhouette in the doorway. His breathing was still labored. "I'm okay." He didn't want her to worry any more than she already was.

His mother crossed the tiny room and sat on the edge of his bed. She was still in her work uniform. "Are you sure? I heard you yell." She ran a gentle hand over his brow. His forehead was dripping with sweat.

"I think it's getting worse," Evan replied hoarsely.

She sighed uneasily. "Do you want me to get you some water?"

He nodded, clearing his throat.

His mother rose and began to leave, then stopped at the door and turned back around. "Do you want me to go with you tomorrow? I can try to get someone to cover for me."

He shook his head. "I'll be okay."

2

Evan wrung his hands and took a deep breath. "It happened again."

She raised her eyebrows. "Again? How many times?"

"Four."

Dr. Shannon Mayer stared at the teenager for a long time. He was sitting in a thick padded leather chair with a nervous look on his face. "When?"

He pushed himself back in the chair. "One last week and two this week. And then another last night."

"Do you want to tell me about them?" she asked calmly.

"I guess so."

Mayer frowned. "Evan, you don't *have* to tell me anything. But I'm here to help you, and I can't do that unless you let me."

Evan shrugged. "I know. There's just not much to say. They're just like the other ones."

"Was it when you went to bed again?"

He nodded. "When I was falling asleep, but they're happening more often now."

Mayer inhaled and stared at him, thinking. "Evan, I think we may need to consider something a bit more . . . aggressive."

"What does that mean, like drugs?"

"A prescription, yes."

Evan didn't answer. He didn't want pills. He'd already told her that. It seemed like everyone at school was on some kind of pill these days. Something to keep you focused. Something to calm you down. Something to make you less moody. He was starting to feel like he was one of the only kids *not* popping something, legal or not. He lowered his voice. "I really don't want to."

"I understand, but if we can't at least get some kind of handle on this, it could become a bigger problem before we diagnose it, which means it will be harder to treat. If these episodes are becoming more frequent, I think we're going to need to act quickly."

He sat quietly in the chair, picking absently at the seam in the dark leather. "Maybe it's like a medical thing," he offered. "You know, instead of psychological. Maybe I just need a little physical therapy, or maybe more broccoli or something."

Mayer's lips curled at his joke. "But not broccoli *pills*."

Evan chuckled. "Right."

"It's possible it could be something medical. But you said you hadn't had any injuries lately. And medical problems like this don't normally happen at the same time of day." She peered at him through her rectangular-framed glasses. "Unless . . . you remember something."

He was pretty sure that was her way of asking if he was lying. He wasn't really, at least not technically. He wasn't lying as much as just keeping something to himself. But if it meant not taking pills, then he'd have to tell her. It was just embarrassing, especially since he'd just turned eighteen.

"Evan?"

He snapped out of his blank stare. "Yes?"

"Did you remember something new?"

The last of Evan's grin disappeared and was followed by a solemn expression. "Uh yeah, I guess I did . . . sort of. There is something I haven't told you . . . exactly."

"And what is that?"

It was only his third session, but something had struck him from the first time he met Dr. Mayer: nothing seemed to surprise her. She always looked at him with the same calm expression. He hoped that meant her other patients were even weirder than he was.

"Well," he began, "it's about when they started."

"When the episodes started?"

"Yeah." He took a breath as she watched him. "This kinda started happening after . . . an accident."

Mayer's brow furrowed. "What kind of accident?"

"A bike accident. I kinda hit a car."

Her eyes opened wider. "You got hit by a car!"

"No." He shook his head. "I, uh, hit the car."

"You hit a car? On your bike?"

"More or less."

Mayer leaned forward, concerned. "How bad was it?"

Evan shrugged. "Well, my bike doesn't work anymore. I have to get a new wheel and fork. The rest of it is still okay, but I guess it's more like a unicycle now."

Mayer managed to keep her eyes from rolling. "Were you hurt!" *God, why didn't he tell me? Was he embarrassed?*

"Not really. Just a lot of scrapes. My helmet was busted though." He decided to leave out limping home in the rain, carrying the bike.

This time Mayer could not stop her eyes from reacting. "Evan, a head injury can be very serious. Why didn't you tell me this?"

His nervous gaze bounced around the room. "I didn't think it was that bad. I only had a headache for a little while."

My God. "Evan, listen to me. We need to get you checked out by a medical doctor. If this paramnesia started as a result of your injury, then it could be significant."

Evan shrugged again. "It was just a headache. I've had them before. My mom thinks they might be stress related, from things at school."

Mayer sighed and leaned back into her own chair. Evan was certainly getting more than his share of being picked on, which unfortunately, due to his demeanor and size at his age, was not entirely surprising. Was it possible this was related to something else? Yes. Was it likely? Not in her opinion. But the fact was, he was officially an adult now. She couldn't actually make him do anything.

"Evan, would you at least let someone take a look at you?"

"How much does that cost?"

Mayer knew they didn't have much money. He told her it was just himself and his mother, and she worked two jobs to keep him in a decent neighborhood and a good school. And judging from the healthcare plan he was on, Mayer suspected their situation was worse than he let on.

She sat for a few moments, quietly thinking. "Evan, will you make a deal with me? If we spend some more time trying to understand these . . . experiences you're having, will you promise me that you'll see a medical doctor if we find anything that suggests they might be related to your crash and not simply stress?" She held up a hand before he could answer. "And don't worry about the cost. We'll figure something out. Okay?"

He relented. "Okay."

"Good." Mayer straightened in her chair. "Then I would like to try something. Can you come back again tomorrow, earlier?"

"I think so."

She rolled the chair to her desk and checked her calendar. She jotted the time on a small appointment card and handed it to him. "How about noon?"

He glanced at the card and then stood up, pushing it into his pants pocket. "School doesn't start again until Monday."

"But listen," Mayer said, standing up with him. "There is something important I want you to do. Actually it's something I want to make sure you *don't* do!"

"Okay." He was not about to ask questions. He was happy to get out of there while he could, before Dr. Mayer asked the question he feared answering. *What was it that caused your bicycle accident?*

3

The San Ysidro Port of Entry—the busiest land border crossing in the world, where over three hundred thousand people commuted between California and Tijuana, Mexico every day. Yet even though it housed the largest border facility in the Americas and employed the highest number of agents, the wait to cross into the United States from Mexico could take as long as five hours on a bad day. And today was one of those days.

Hundreds of cars sat idly in the hot afternoon sun, waiting for the line to advance, many with their windows up and air conditioners on. Near the front of the line, over two dozen lanes stretched the length of the three-story structure where border patrol agents asked drivers questions and looked over their cars.

Silently, a fifty-year-old man studied two agents from behind the steering wheel of his old silver Honda Accord. He watched carefully as the agents questioned the driver of the car in front of him. It was taking longer than usual. He wondered if they were looking for something, or someone, specific. He gripped the wheel tighter, waiting.

Finally, the car pulled away, and as the man was motioned forward, one of the agents mumbled something to his partner. The man inched forward and tried to breathe calmly.

"Afternoon," the agent said, leaning in.

The man put the sedan in park and handed the agent his driver's license.

The agent took the ID and looked it over. "You live in Santa Clarita?"

"Yes."

The second agent on the other side of the car peered through the front side window, then walked back and looked into the back seat.

"What was the reason for visiting Mexico?" the first agent asked.

"To visit my sister. She's sick," he lied.

"And where does your sister live?"

"Rosarito."

The agent pursed his lips and nodded slightly. "Are you bringing anything back?"

The driver shook his bald head. "No." He was desperately trying to appear as calm as possible. There wasn't anything in the car; they could search it all day long. *As long as they didn't search him.*

"Did you bring anything in, Mr. Roa?" asked the agent, glancing back to his ID.

"Nope," he lied again. *Was his expression still calm? Was he overcompensating?*

A beep sounded and the agent looked at the small device in his hand. The sedan's license plate flashed on the screen, which displayed the date and time the car had last crossed through from the U.S., a little over five hours ago. The agent straightened and exchanged looks with his partner over the top of the vehicle. His partner gave a silent nod of his head.

"Okay." He handed the license back to the driver. "Welcome back, Mr. Roa."

Roa nodded and pulled forward, slowly accelerating and joining the narrowing stream of inbound U.S. traffic. He looked in the rearview mirror and watched the agents turn their attention to the next car. He thought about how lucky he was that the hot weather made the beads of sweat on his forehead appear normal. Finally, he patted his breast pocket to make sure it was still there. He was lucky indeed.

Roa looked at his watch and mentally calculated the time back to Santa Clarita. This was the longest he'd been away in over eighteen months, and he was getting very nervous.

4

As it turned out, what Dr. Mayer didn't want Evan to do was sleep.

She told him to do whatever he had to do to stay awake. Fortunately he had an old video game at home, and since they were out for spring break, there was no school to get up for. Needless to say, he was exhausted.

"Are you tired?" she asked with a hint of amusement. She knew what he had been doing all night.

Evan let his head roll back against the top of the padded chair. "Very."

Mayer crossed the room and stood next to the long psychiatrist's couch. "Can you lie down here please?"

Evan complied as she picked up a clipboard and rolled her chair over, next to the couch. "Evan, what I'd like to do today is to see if we can elicit one of these experiences as you drift off to sleep. Of course, I hope you're not too tired," she added as an afterthought. "I want you to make yourself comfortable."

She wrote some things on her pad of paper and lowered the clipboard. "What I want to do is look for anything that may signal any kind of physiological distress. For example, things that might tell us whether these episodes are related to your injury, like mild shaking, blackouts, or drooling."

"Drooling!"

"It's just an example. Now lean back and close your eyes. Try to relax." He felt her fingertips touch his arm. "I'm also going to measure your heart rate a few times. I'll try not to make it too distracting."

"Okay." Evan wriggled his body and tried to settle into the soft couch. He was really tired. It only took a few minutes to feel his eyelids getting heavy. His disjointed thoughts, the sure sign of nodding off, were the last thing he remembered.

—•—

Suddenly Evan bolted upright in a cold sweat, a panicked look on his face.

"Easy! Easy!" Mayer said from her chair next to him.

He turned to see her gently holding his wrist. "What happened?" he asked, gasping for air. "How long . . . was I out?"

Mayer looked down at her watch. "Almost four minutes." She stared at him, observing closely as he blinked and became silent. "Did you see anything?"

It took Evan a full minute to calm his breathing and answer. "Yes." He could still see it, and it was as clear as a bell. These didn't fade as quickly as dreams did. Unfortunately they stayed for a long time.

Mayer studied him as he lay back down, mindful to prod gently. She waited until he looked at her. "And what did you see?"

"I saw . . . us. I saw the two of us, sitting here. I was on the couch, and you were sitting next to me."

"You mean just as we are now?"

"Yes."

Mayer considered Evan's answer. "Did this feel like one of the episodes, or were you just remembering what you had last seen?"

"No," he said, shaking his head. "It definitely wasn't a memory."

"Are you sure? How do you know?"

Evan turned and looked at her, then glanced at the corner of her office near the window. "Because I saw us from over there."

———•———

Mayer sat in her chair, silently staring out the window. She was struggling to concentrate, even on Evan, whose problem was clearly getting worse. She forced herself to focus.

She had to admit to herself that his "over there" statement struck her as a little odd. But the more she thought about it, the more sense it made. It was not uncommon for patients to imagine things from a distance or a different angle. In fact, it happened quite often.

Frankly, imagining the two of them sitting across the room was rather benign, even when he added that he saw the reception area where Mayer's receptionist was eating lunch. He had just walked through there. Not to mention the boy was eighteen, and Shannon Mayer's receptionist was exceptionally attractive. No mystery there. But clinically speaking, misperceiving stimuli was one thing, and it was called an *illusion*. Seeing something that wasn't there at all was something else: a *hallucination*, and that was of far more concern. That Evan seemed to be experiencing the former, and not the latter, gave her some sense of relief.

Hallucinations were often symptoms of very real problems. Drug and alcohol use were well-known causes, but hallucinations could also be the result of genuine mental or physical illness. She was convinced Evan didn't drink or take drugs, which left the alternative diagnosis a much more worrying one, especially with a head injury involved.

What really worried her, though, was how quickly Evan's heart rate had increased; she was worried even more by how quickly he began sweating. Both effects were unusual, as was the shaking, and while together they weren't enough for her to believe he'd been having epileptic episodes, Mayer reluctantly acknowledged that might yet be the reason for his hallucinations.

A few minutes later, Evan returned from the restroom, closing the door quietly behind him. He walked tentatively across the room, not sure if he should sit back down.

Mayer answered his unspoken question by standing up to meet him. "Evan, I'm going to suggest we end our examination early, after what you've just been through. I want you to go home and try to get some sleep."

"Okay." There was obvious relief in his voice.

"With that said, I think I *would* like you to see a doctor. I think this problem may still be related to your accident."

Evan took a deep breath.

"And I don't want you to worry about money, let me work on that." She motioned toward the door, and walked with him.

"I don't want any pills."

"I understand." *This was not the time to get into that*, she thought.

She opened the door, and they walked back down the short hallway into the large, open reception area. Mayer kept her grin hidden as she watched Evan's expression change upon seeing her receptionist, Tania. She could have been a model, and most of her male patients had a very similar reaction.

"Tania," she said, "could you please call Dr. Wells at Family Medical and tell him I'd like to send someone over as soon as possible?" She looked at Evan. "Can you make it Friday?"

Evan shrugged. "I think so."

Tania dialed the number and spoke briefly to someone on the other end, while Evan tried hard not to stare at her.

She hung up and wrote the time and address on a card. "Do you know where Cypress Street is?"

"Yes." Evan took the card from Tania and examined it.

"Do you have a way to get there?" Mayer interjected.

Evan shrugged and snuck another glance at Tania. "If I can't catch the bus, I guess there's always parachuting in."

Tania laughed and flashed her perfect smile.

At the same time, Mayer chuckled and put a gentle hand on Evan's arm. "Let's talk again after you've seen Dr. Wells."

Evan thanked them and crossed the room to the door, opened it and stepped out.

When the door clicked shut, Mayer turned to her receptionist. "Thanks Tania. Can you be sure to schedule a call with Evan on Monday?"

"Sure, no problem."

Mayer took a deep breath, still thinking about the young man. As she turned to walk back to her office, something on Tania's desk sent a chill through the doctor's body.

5

Roa sat down at his old kitchen table. It was made of green Formica with matching vinyl seats, and easily recognizable by anyone who lived through the 1960s or '70s. The rest of the small dining room was cluttered with boxes and piles of magazines stacked around the base of the walls. A tired-looking computer sat in the corner on a desk that seemed almost as old as the kitchen table. In a few days, it would all be gone.

He unfolded an envelope and carefully pulled out the contents. Obtaining fake passports was not easy, especially if you wanted them to work. He looked at both and studied the pictures again. He flexed the tiny pages back and forth. They looked good, really good.

It took him almost a year to find someone who could counterfeit this well; and it took more than just a lot of money, it took time. He knew he'd found the right group when they proceeded to spend months investigating *him*, making sure his request wasn't a set-up. Not that people in China had all that much to worry about. But ultimately, the most important benefit was avoiding the biggest mistake people made when dealing with forged documents.

Most people in the United States interested in buying a new ID simply didn't know what they were doing. They didn't understand how the system worked or what was necessary. As a result, most of them made the same classic blunder, because they were unable to think outside the box. They were never able to get out of the mindset of a U.S. citizen. In other words, the idiots only considered a new U.S.-issued identity, which is why so many were caught. Creating a new ID in the U.S. meant also breaking into the systems of the State Department, which virtually no one could do, regardless of what the forgers claimed. But by then they already had your money.

What a select few realized was that it was far easier to break into a computer system in a smaller, less sophisticated country instead. For example, in Roa's case, Belize. And only idiots would send forged documents through the U.S. mail.

He hadn't wanted to go to Mexico to retrieve them, but it was the safest way, and in the end would be well worth it.

Roa looked at the picture on the second passport. It looked good, very relaxed. She would do fine. And their exit point sure as hell wasn't going to be Mexico. This time it would be the weakest point of the entire United States border. And it would be soon.

6

Glendale, California was founded by José María Verdugo in the late eighteenth century as part of a large grant from then Governor Diego de Borica. Over two hundred years later, the city's oldest building, the Verdugo Adobe, was still standing, and Glendale had grown into one of the largest suburbs in the greater Los Angeles area. The area also had the honor of having the second largest number of psychiatrists in the country. Some joked that given the reputation of the L.A. area and nearby Hollywood, the high number of local psychiatrists was not a coincidence.

The Verdugo Adobe was just two blocks away when Shannon Mayer drove by on Canada Boulevard. She continued north for another quarter mile, then turned left and headed west on San Gabriel. After a slow right turn, she passed the entrance of the country club and continued up the winding hill, inevitably driving slower and slower.

She was still thinking about Evan. He was a good kid, quiet, but very sharp. She had to admit he'd become a strange, yet welcome, distraction for her. But as her car made its way up the winding road, that distraction quickly melted away.

Reaching the top, she slowed at the end of the cul-de-sac and brought her blue BMW X5 to a stop. A long stare at the iron gates filled her with a familiar dread. She reluctantly reached up to press the button on her visor. Both sides of the white gates swung open smoothly, allowing her to pull through onto a long paved drive-way. Mayer barely noticed the manicured lawn as she rolled slowly up the driveway, finally stopping at the far end in front of a beauti-ful house. The red brick face with white columns on either side of the entryway gave it an old, colonial-style appearance, and it was the first thing she had fallen in love with.

Mayer put the car in park and turned off the ignition, but she did not get out. She stared wearily at the giant house and took a long, deep breath. Just a few years ago this was her dream house; but now, coming home was very different. It was agonizing, and the last thing she wanted to do was go inside.

7

The office on Cypress Street was just off of South Glendale Avenue. It was a small group of private medical doctors, practicing just a few blocks from the local hospital and less than a half mile from Shannon Mayer's own office. It also happened to be where Mayer's younger sister worked.

"Hey Sis," Mary said when she spotted her older sister through the narrow doorway. "I didn't know you were coming over." She shook her hands over the small sink and reached for a paper towel. "We had a look at your boy this morning. Evan Nash, right?"

Shannon nodded. "How'd it go?"

Mary finished, tossing the towel away, and smiled at her. "I'm not supposed to say. Doctor Wells wanted to brief you. Or should I say, *John* wanted to brief you."

Shannon tried to hide her rolling eyes, but her sister caught it anyway. It was well known that the doctor had a crush on her. After a couple of dates many years before, Shannon had given him the old "let's be friends" line. He was disappointed, but he never seemed to lose his interest in her. Mary had teased her incessantly over the years, suggesting that the good Dr. Wells may just be trying to wait out Shannon's marriage.

Of course it was harmless and even a tad advantageous from time to time. This was one of those times. Knowing that Evan didn't have insurance, she asked John Wells if he would do her a favor and have a look at him. Not surprisingly, Wells was more than happy to help. Crushes, even innocent ones, have their perks.

Hearing that Shannon was in the office, the doctor wrapped things up with a patient and hustled down the hall, finding the sisters both in the last examination room. "Well, hello Shannon. What a pleasant surprise," he exclaimed with a delighted grin.

She smiled back as he gave her a hug. "Hi John, how are you?"

"Always better when I see you," he said with a wink. "I take it you came in to talk about your young Mr. Nash. I had a look at him this morning."

Shannon wasn't in the chattiest of moods, but she played along. "Listen John, I really appreciate your help. He doesn't have very good insurance, and I didn't know who else to ask."

"Oh no, not at all." Wells waved it off. "Anything for you, Shannon."

"Well, thank you. You're very sweet."

Wells beamed even wider. "I can't disagree with you there."

Shannon gave him a courteous laugh. "So how did it go? Did you find anything?"

"Actually, yes." Wells furrowed his brows. "Did he tell you that he'd been in a serious bicycle accident?"

"He told me about the accident, but he didn't indicate that it was particularly bad."

"Well, it was," Wells said. He was surprised when Mary slipped Evan's file into his hands. Shannon's sister stepped back, still enjoying the exchange.

"Thanks Mary." As Wells opened the file, Shannon stepped in closer to peer at it. "I think the boy had a concussion."

"A concussion!"

Wells nodded. "Yes. It was a pretty hard fall. Said he had a headache for a couple days."

"A couple of days!" Shannon was incredulous.

"He didn't tell you any of this?"

"Not this, no." She frowned. "It seems he's still holding back on me. How is he now?"

"Well, that's the good part. He appears to be fine now. No long-term symptoms, which is good, although his blood pressure was a bit high. But that's pretty normal for new patients."

"So nothing else at all?"

Wells shook his head. "Not that I could find. Other than getting shaken up by the accident, he doesn't appear any worse for the wear. Everything else looks normal."

"Thank God."

"So," Wells said, smiling again. He held the file underneath as he folded his arms. "On another note, I'm afraid this favor is going to cost you a lunch."

"Is that right?" Shannon forced a grin.

"And this time you can't say no."

"Oh, alright," she said in playful tone. "But you need to give me a couple weeks. Things are pretty hectic."

"Take your time," he said. "I know things have been tough for you. As always, if there's anything you need, you know we're all here for you."

Shannon gave his arm a sincere pat. "Thanks."

"Okay, I've got to go. Don't forget to call me." Wells gave her a quick hug goodbye and headed back down the hall.

Shannon turned to her sister, who was still smiling. "You just eat that up, don't you?"

"I do," Mary said, laughing. "I really, really do."

Shannon stood watching her with a sarcastic expression. "When you're done laughing, I have something I need to talk to you about."

Mary topped off the small jar of cotton swabs and put the larger container back up in the cabinet. "Okay, okay, go ahead."

Shannon reached back and gently closed the door. "This is just between you and me, all right?"

Her sister watched her curiously. "All right."

"It's about that boy Evan that came in. There's something strange going on."

"What do you mean?"

Shannon thought for a moment. "He's been having these illusions lately; at least I thought they were illusions. Now I'm not so sure. But he said they all started after that bicycle accident."

"So you think they're related to the accident."

"Yes."

Mary instinctively looked at the door the doctor had just walked out of. "Well, John did say he had a concussion. I suppose even with everything else looking normal, things like reflexes and pupil dilation, there could still be a lingering problem."

"But that's just a possibility, not a probability."

"Well yeah," Mary nodded. "Kids tend to bounce back pretty quickly from these things, and I have to say, while the kid is a little shy, he seemed fine to me. No delayed responses, no slurring, nothing. What kind of illusions is he having?"

Shannon sighed. "That's the weird part. They're not strange or twisted; they're . . . actually more like him just hanging out in his bedroom."

Mary gave her a puzzled look. "Hanging out in his room? That sounds more like daydreaming."

"Well, that's what I wanted to talk to you about," Shannon said. "I'm worried they might be something more serious, like hallucinations. Something happened the other day that I can't explain."

Mary raised her eyebrows expectantly.

"He had one of these episodes in my office on Wednesday, when I had him lying down. It only lasted a few minutes but part of it was very strange."

"Strange how?"

Shannon hesitated as she thought about it. "He saw a couple of things. One was the two of us in the room, from a distance. Which isn't that unusual," she added. "But it's what he said next that has me a little freaked out. He said he briefly saw the room out front and my assistant Tania eating lunch."

"And that's weird because . . ."

"Because she wasn't eating lunch when he came into the office."

Mary shrugged. "So what. The kid fantasized about her eating lunch or maybe taking her to lunch. I mean come on, have you *looked* at Tania? I'm sure all of your male patients have spent some time thinking about her. It sounds to me like this Evan kid has a little thing for her. He *is* eighteen, which means he probably has more testosterone coursing through him right now than blood."

"I thought the same thing," Shannon said, shaking her head. "Except for two problems; one is that he wasn't in that picture with her. In fact, he said he saw her just sitting at her desk. And two, that was the first time he'd come into the office that early in the day. He normally comes late in the afternoon after school, which means he always talked to Emily, my other assistant who works later. In other words, Evan had never *met* Tania until that day."

"So, he had a fantasy about a pretty girl he just met."

Shannon shook her head. "Fantasies like that tend to be conscious thoughts, not unconscious, unless it's a dream. And this didn't seem to be either."

"Hmm." Mary gnawed absentmindedly, though gently, on her bottom lip, thinking. "Okay, so he has his first appointment around lunchtime and walks in to see Tania at her desk with her lunch, still not a big deal."

Shannon shook her head again. "That's what I'm trying to say. Tania didn't even *have* her lunch when he came in. She went out to get something after he was already in my office."

Mary's eyes opened a little wider.

Shannon continued. "So she didn't have a lunch until after his appointment had started, but when she did, she was eating it about the same time that Evan had his hallucination." She paused and took a short breath. "And there's something else."

"What?"

Shannon gave her sister a confused look. "When Evan was in my office and told me what he'd seen, he never actually used the word lunch. What he said was *sandwich*, which was exactly what she'd gotten."

Mary was suddenly speechless. After a long pause she finally replied. "So . . . what do you want me to do?"

Shannon lowered her voice. "I want you to help me with something."

8

The Glendale Beeline Bus stopped at the corner of Brand and Magnolia and swung its doors open with a loud pressurized hiss. A few seconds later, Evan descended the steps and hopped down onto the concrete sidewalk.

He squinted under the bright sun and looked around before dropping his old skateboard in front of him. It was already getting warm and his long-sleeved T-shirt was not helping, but he preferred these shirts, even in late spring, because of his slight frame.

The bus closed its doors and drove onward as Evan pushed off and coasted around the tight corner, continuing down Magnolia Avenue. Traffic near the hospital was light on Saturday mornings since most residents headed toward the city's outdoor mall instead, but he still had to zigzag around a few cars as they pulled out.

He suddenly stopped and jumped to the side as a gold-colored Mercedes Benz roared out of a long driveway, nearly hitting him. When it lurched to a stop, Evan saw two young teenagers laughing at him. He recognized both from school. The passenger leaned out the window, peering down at the old wooden skateboard. He turned and said something to the driver, who snickered loudly. With a final smirk, they hit the gas and peeled out into the street.

As Evan watched them speed away, he heard a sound behind him and turned to see a small, yapping dog run after the car. Behind the dog stood a young girl with an empty hand outstretched. A look of panic covered her face as the small terrier ran after the car, headed for the busy street.

Evan lunged at the passing dog and dropped his foot down onto the long leash, halting the terrier just a few feet from the end of the driveway. He gently reached down and scooped up the tiny dog, then walked back to the girl just as her grandmother came trotting up behind her. Evan approached slowly and handed the dog to the girl. She immediately wrapped her hands around the animal and rubbed her nose against the back of its small head.

The woman looked lovingly at her granddaughter, then up to Evan. "Thank you, young man!"

Evan nodded and smiled at the girl. "You're welcome." With that, he calmly turned and walked back to the street to retrieve his skateboard. He didn't notice the girl whisper something to her grandmother behind him.

Turning the board over with his foot, he glanced up just in time to see the small girl run up to him, the dog still in her arms. Without a word, she shyly held something out to him. Evan lowered his hand and she dropped a shiny quarter into his palm.

"Thank you," she said meekly and ran back to her waiting grandmother.

Evan watched her run back and then gazed down at his reward. He smiled and slid it into his pocket.

As he continued along the sidewalk, Evan thought about the boys in the car. They were the ones responsible for his accident. They'd thought it was funny when they cut him off on his bike, causing him to crash into a parked car. They thought it was even funnier when they told everyone at school.

He'd been getting harassed for years. Was it because he was short? Because he was quiet? He'd never bothered anyone and yet they kept at it. And now his bike was smashed, he had to see multiple doctors, and his health was in danger. All because of their sick enjoyment of picking on someone.

No more.

——•——

Her office was two blocks farther down Magnolia. Evan climbed the stone stairs and stopped in front of the second door on the right, knocking lightly. He almost knocked again when Dr. Mayer opened the door from the other side. The small building was deathly quiet; the offices were closed on Saturdays. Shannon smiled politely at Evan and motioned him in.

They made their way down the hallway and entered her office, where Evan sat down on the couch and watched Shannon close the door.

She pulled up her chair and sat down next to him. "How are you, Evan?"

"Pretty good."

"How do you feel?"

"Okay, I guess. I slept last night but only a little."

Shannon nodded. "So you go back to school on Monday?"

"Yeah."

She watched him, studying his body language. He clearly wasn't looking forward to returning to school, even though the year was almost over. "I take it you're still getting harassed?"

He shrugged.

"Same boys?"

Evan shrugged again. "There's a lot of 'em."

Shannon gave a sympathetic nod. Recent laws obligated her to report instances of harassment at school. But she wasn't sure how effective that would be; it could make matters worse. She also didn't know whether the law applied to kids who were technically legal adults. She frowned before raising an eyebrow. "So what do you think you're going to do?"

"I don't know. I think I've had enough."

"What do you mean?"

"That's why my accident happened. Because I never stood up to them."

Mayer gave him a smile. She'd suspected as much. "I hope you're not planning to do something irresponsible."

"Nah."

She nodded, and decided not to press it. Instead, she changed the subject. "So do you know why I asked you to come in today?"

"Because of the visions?"

"That's right." She crossed one leg over the other. "Is that okay?"

He nodded. "Yeah."

Shannon withheld a wry smile. He wasn't too talkative this morning. "Evan, I need to ask you something before we begin."

"Okay."

"After the dream you had here the other day, I'm a little concerned about you, physically. What I mean is that your body reacted very strangely last time, which worries me if we're going to try to learn what this is. Do you understand what I'm saying?"

"You're worried something might happen to me?"

"That's right." She nodded. *He was a sharp kid.* "Which is why I wanted a doctor to look at you."

"What did he say?"

"He said you looked fine. But you *did* have a concussion. Do you know what that is?"

Evan thought a moment. "A head injury?"

"That's right. It's a head injury, and while it's not necessarily permanent, it can cause people to black out for a little while or have trouble focusing later. Do you remember if you blacked out when you had your accident?"

Evan tried to remember. "I don't . . . think so. It all happened pretty fast, but I don't remember blacking out."

Shannon nodded again. "Well just to be safe, I'd like to ask your permission to have someone join us for these exercises, to help me."

"Who?"

"My sister. She's a nurse and works for the doctor you saw yesterday. I'd like her to help me keep an eye on you and make sure we don't have any problems." Her next words were deliberate. "As your counselor, Evan, I have a responsibility to keep you safe. Do you understand what I'm saying?"

Evan nodded his head. "I think so. This is the only way we can do it?"

"I'm afraid so. Is that okay with you?"

This time a small grin crept across Evan's face. "Is she nice?"

Shannon managed a smile. "Well, I didn't always think so when we were younger." She stood up, out of her chair. "Wait right here."

Shannon walked to the door and opened it. She stuck her head out and called to Mary. A few moments later, she stepped back and held the door open.

Mary came through the door and smiled at Evan. Her blonde hair was pulled back into a ponytail. "Hi Evan. I'm Mary."

"Hi."

"Do you remember me from the office yesterday?"

"Yes," he replied with a small grin.

"Good." Mary walked to the couch and put down a large bag. "I'll try not to get in the way too much. Can I have you lie back and relax?"

As he did, Evan looked back and forth at the two curiously. He hadn't noticed the resemblance yesterday, but it was obvious now seeing them next to each other. "Who's older?" he asked.

Mary feigned a look of shock and looked back at Shannon. With a chuckle, Mary turned back and reached into the bag, pulling out a small, box-shaped device, which she placed on a nearby table. She pulled the table closer to the couch. She then turned on the device and waited for the display to light up while she unwound a small wire with what looked like a finger splint on the end. She gently slid this over Evan's left index finger.

"This will keep track of your pulse and oxygen level. It's not too uncomfortable, is it?"

He shook his head. "Nope."

"Good." She turned to the small device, which was now displaying a group of numbers, and firmly pressed a button. The numbers reset and a few moments later displayed his current levels. Next, Mary placed a long thin strip on his forehead. "And this is for your temperature." Finally, she pulled out the familiar thick blood pressure cuff with a bulb attached and wrapped it around his upper arm.

Behind her sister, Shannon quietly pulled down the shades on the opposite wall, darkening the room. She sat back in her chair next to Evan and waited for Mary to finish taking his blood pressure. "Okay, Evan, what I'd like to do is see if we can repeat what happened the other day. Do you think you can do that again?"

"I'll try."

Shannon reached over and grabbed a clipboard off her desk. "So tell me, exactly how much sleep *did* you get last night?"

"Just a little," he replied quietly. "They're happening almost every night now."

Shannon and Mary silently exchanged looks.

"Well, let's just see if we can do something about that," Shannon said with a wink. "Now Evan, I'd like you to think about the corner of the room like you did the other day. But this time, I want to tell you that I had Mary tape a piece of paper to the back of my desk chair. If you think you can see it, I want you to tell me what color you think the paper is."

Evan looked a little puzzled. "Okay."

What she didn't tell him was that she had also laid a colored piece of paper on her desk in plain view. It was a common psychiatrist's trick for testing subliminal associations. If Evan claimed to see the paper on the back of the chair but reported the same color as the paper on her desk, it could reveal whether his visions were really occurring on a subconscious level or based on environmental stimuli.

After nearly ten minutes of silence, Evan's eyes finally closed. His head relaxed and settled deeper into the thick cushion. His heartbeat descended into the low sixties and his breathing gradually slowed.

It was just a few minutes more before the steady beeping of Mary's monitor changed. Both women looked at the display.

"His pulse just jumped to ninety!" Mary whispered. She continued watching, surprised again as the number passed 100. She quietly pumped more air into the cuff and measured his blood pressure again. His systolic pressure was still barely within the normal range, but her eyes opened wide when she noticed the strip on his forehead. It was changing colors.

Mary quickly, but gently, touched Evan's hand. She looked worriedly at Shannon, and in an urgent whisper, told her: "He's losing body heat fast!" She checked his blood pressure again. It was also falling quickly. Correction, it was *plunging*!

She looked worriedly to Shannon. "Something's wrong!"

"What is it?"

"I don't know!" Now her whisper was frantic. "We have to wake him up!"

Shannon leaned forward. "Right now?"

"Right now!"

Shannon was immediately out of her seat. She grasped Evan's left hand causing the small monitor to fall from his finger. "Evan!" She said aloud, "Evan!"

He did not respond. His chest began to move erratically.

"Evan!" she said louder. "Evan, wake up!" She slapped his face lightly. "Evan, can you hear me?"

Mary gasped when his pulse passed 120. She stood up quickly and pushed Shannon out of the way. She held nothing back, slapping him hard and yelling, *"Evan! Wake up!"*

Just as Mary was about to hit him again, Evan suddenly jerked his head. His eyes fluttered and began to open as he instinctively brought his hand up, trying to regain his bearings. He opened his left eye first, blinking repeatedly, followed by his right. He brought his hand the rest of the way up and over his eyes to block the light that Shannon had just turned on.

Mary grabbed his left hand and pressed her fingertips against his wrist. His pulse was slowing. She pumped more air into the cuff. His blood pressure was also rising.

"Evan, can you hear me?" Shannon asked.

"Yes," he said slowly. He shut his eyes again hard then reopened them. He tilted his head up, searching for the source of her voice. When he found her, Evan furrowed his brow. "What happened?"

Shannon patted his shoulder and tried to smile. "You just got us a little worried."

"Oh." Evan lowered his head to the couch and squinted toward the ceiling. After a long pause, he looked back up at her. "Who's Roy Rogers?"

9

Shannon made sure Evan was asleep before quietly closing the door. She exhaled slowly, turned around, and walked back down the short hallway to where Mary was waiting.

Mary wasted no time letting Shannon know how she felt. "What the hell was that?" She thrust the piece of pink paper at Shannon.

Shannon didn't answer. She simply stared at the paper that had been taped to the back of her chair.

"Well?" Mary folded her arms, waiting. "Are you going to tell me?"

"I just wanted to see . . . "

"You're one of the most analytical people I know. You've never gone for this kind of thing! Why would you . . ." Her eyes grew large as she realized what was happening. "Oh my God! This isn't about that kid at all, is it? This is about *Ellie!*"

Shannon didn't reply. She lowered her head and eventually began to shake it from side to side. "I'm losing it, Mary. I mean it. I am really *losing* it!"

Mary froze.

"I can't take it," Shannon said, quivering. "I just can't take it. It's *killing* me!" Her eyes began to tear up. "It's not getting better, it's getting worse, and I am barely holding it all together!"

Mary stammered, "B-but I thought . . ."

"It's *not* getting better," she repeated. "It's just a mirage, a facade that I put on to try to get through each and every day. And it's just me . . . all by myself, trying to hold everything together—the bills, the house, the practice."

"What about Dennis?"

Shannon shook her head again and wiped the tears from her eyes. "He barely talks to me anymore. He barely talks at all. He hardly eats anything. He just sits there wallowing, wasting away and letting it fill him like a terrible disease. And you know what?" She looked helplessly at her sister. "It's filling me too, and I can't stop it. Every day is worse, and even though it's supposed to get better, it isn't! It's all I can do just to make it through the day."

She backed up against the wall and covered her face with her hands. "God, the worst part is waking up. It's the worst torture you can imagine. For just a split second you forget; you forget and think it was all a dream, and then immediately it hits you like a train again. It wasn't a dream, it's real, and it's even worse than it was yesterday."

Mary wrapped her arm around Shannon's and let her sister's head fall against her shoulder.

"Sis, I don't know what to do. I'm at the end of my rope, and I don't know how much longer I can hang on."

Tears began to run from Mary's eyes as she pressed her cheek against her sister's hair. She didn't know what to say, so she didn't say anything at all.

After several minutes, Shannon managed to regain her composure and wipe more tears away. With her head still against Mary, she eyed the pink paper in her hand. She took a deep breath, then reached out and took the paper, holding it out and studying it.

"I know we agreed on this test to disprove the hallucinations, or prove they were subliminal, or whatever. But before Evan walked in, it suddenly hit me. We weren't doing anything to see if they were *real*." She shrugged. "Look, I know I'm a psychiatrist and I'm the analytical one, but . . . what if they *are* real? What if he can see things? What if he could help?"

Mary couldn't hide her look of surprise, nor the look of sympathy that followed.

"Am I crazy?" Shannon cried. "Am I just some desperate mother hoping for a miracle no matter how irrational it seems? Or is it at least possible? I mean if he can see things, maybe he could see . . . *other* things?"

Mary frowned. From the beginning, she had been unable to even imagine the horror her sister had to go through over the last year and a half, and now to find out the pain was even worse felt like a dagger through her own heart. She reached out and took her sister's hand. "Anything is possible."

Shannon forced a grin. "I'm not sure who is more skeptical now, you or me."

Mary shook her head. "Not me, not on this. Remember who you're talking to. I was an ER nurse for seven years. I've seen things happen that no one could explain. I mean strange things. No, I'm not claiming anything is impossible here."

After a long silence, Mary glanced at the paper in Shannon's hand. "So why did you choose that name?"

Shannon sniffed again and wiped away more tears. "Well, we knew that if he said the paper was pink it would indicate something subconscious. But if they weren't hallucinations and what he was seeing was *real*, then I needed a way to know. So I wrote a name on the paper that would be easy to read but one he'd probably never heard before."

Mary smirked. "And you picked Roy Rogers."

"He was Dad's favorite."

Mary nodded her head reluctantly. "Well, maybe this kid Evan can help you, and maybe he can't. But you're *going* to tell him. You're going to tell him because he needs to understand. And let me tell you something else: exam or no exam, what just happened in there, I have *never* seen before. I don't know what's going on with this kid, but it's dangerous!"

10

Mary climbed the steps of the large office building and walked past an ornate fountain near the main entrance. As she reached the glass entry doors, she saw the reflection of the ten-story UCLA Medical Center building across the way.

Established in 1955 and later renamed the Ronald Reagan UCLA Medical Center, it was the most prominent medical center and hospital in all of Southern California. The building Mary had just entered belonged to Latham and Brown, one of the most distinguished law firms in Los Angeles County, and they represented the medical center exclusively. It was no surprise that it was located close by.

She stepped off the elevator onto the third floor and was taken aback by how many people were working on a Saturday. Then again, given their stature, maybe she should not have been surprised. The lobby was impressive, with spotless marble floors and tall pillars on either side of the wide entrance. To the left was a circular wraparound desk with a receptionist sitting behind it.

"Hello, can I help you?" she asked, greeting Mary.

"Yes, thank you. I'm here to see Sue Bales."

The receptionist looked at her screen. "Ah yes, you must be Mary Creece." She typed something into her computer and stood up. "If you'll please follow me," she said, with a polite gesture. She led Mary through the open area, past several glass-fronted offices. Upon reaching the wall, they turned right and headed toward the far corner office.

The receptionist knocked gently on the door that read "S. Bales" and stuck her head inside to make sure she was ready for Mary.

A moment later, Mary walked in with a smile on her face as Sue Bales rose from behind her desk. "Mary!" she cried, and came around to give her a hug.

"Wow, look at you!" Mary replied, squeezing her tight. "I like the new location."

Sue shrugged. "Ah, we pay too much for it, but it has a nice view." She motioned at the floor-to-ceiling glass windows behind her.

"Not bad. How the heck have you been?" Mary glanced around the rest of the office and noted the two walls with tall bookshelves behind her, packed with large, thick medical books and journals. Some were so wide, she wondered how the bindings were strong enough to keep them together.

"Good, how about you? How're Rick and the boys?"

"They're great," Mary said, smiling again. "How about you guys? I was expecting to have to meet you at a soccer game."

"Nah," Sue laughed. "Johnny stopped playing when he got to high school, and Kelli discovered boys about the same time."

"Oh, dear."

Sue rolled her eyes. "No kidding. Come on, have a seat." She pulled out two chairs from in front of her desk and turned them to face each other. "So to what on earth do I owe the pleasure? It must be important if you drove straight down here; not to mention you sounded a little cryptic on the phone."

"Sorry, I wasn't trying to be. I'm just trying to figure something out and was hoping I might be able to get your help."

The two women had been close friends since their nursing school days together. But not long after graduating, their careers parted ways when Sue realized she'd made a mistake. Nursing was not necessarily her forte, but something else was: research, medical research to be exact. And not medical research as it was known today, such as developing new drugs.

Even before she quit nursing, Sue had developed a peculiar habit of finding arcane details relating to rare illnesses: facts that ultimately saved several lives, but also embarrassed some very prestigious doctors. Shortly after one doctor was almost sued as a result of her research, Sue was officially encouraged to pursue those skills *outside* her nursing career, or somewhere else entirely.

However, Sue soon found a match made in heaven—medical litigation. She'd been at it ever since, and her reputation for finding obscure and often case-winning facts was downright legendary.

After catching up, Mary explained in detail Evan's strange experiences and the frightening symptoms she had witnessed in him just hours earlier. When she described what Evan claimed to *see* during the experience, Sue leaned forward with deepening interest.

She raised her eyebrows, intrigued. "He saw the paper *and* the writing on it?"

Mary nodded with her own look of amazement.

"And how low did this kid's temperature get?"

"Ninety-six."

"Wow." Sue's eyes opened even wider, and she leaned back in her chair. "That fast?"

"I've never seen anything like it."

"How fast did his temperature recover after he woke up?"

"Almost as fast. But I have to tell you, it sure scared the hell out of me."

"I can imagine." Sue's eyes narrowed slightly as she thought over the information. "I have to admit I've never heard of anything like this. The heart rate and blood pressure make sense, but that temperature drop . . . and you said he was sweating too, all in three minutes?"

"I haven't seen that kind of sweat in a sauna. And yes," Mary confirmed, "three and a half minutes, tops."

"And he's okay now?"

"He seems to be."

Sue folded her arms. "Well, speaking strictly from a physiology standpoint, those signs don't mix. In fact, I'd say they're almost polar opposites, which makes me think that kid was in some serious trouble. He's darn lucky you slapped him out of it."

Mary gently nodded her head. "I haven't been that scared in a long time."

Sue smiled. "And that's saying something with your background." She shifted in her seat. "Let me ask you this: do you think this paper test of yours could have been in any way, I don't know . . ." She shrugged. "Coincidental?"

Mary thought the question over, even though she'd just spent the last forty-five minutes contemplating it in the car. "Anything is possible, but I can't imagine how. I've tried to think of any possible way—a reflection, subtle or subconscious clues—I just can't think of anything. I really have no idea how else he could have done it."

"Very strange." Sue rested her elbow on the chair's arm and brought her hand up to her face, tapping her finger against her cheek. "Regardless of what might be going on in his head, it sure seems like his body was trying to do everything it could to kill him." A wry expression spread across her face as she looked back at Mary. "And you said you're looking for help."

"Well, 'hoping' might be a better word. I just can't help but wonder whether there's anything like this on the books; maybe some person with similar symptoms, a study, anything."

"Well, I've certainly never heard of it, but that's not exactly definitive." Sue stood up. "I'll spend some time on it."

Mary breathed an audible sigh of relief. "Thank you, Sue. I hate to dump this on you, but I'm pretty worried."

Her friend smiled. "And now I am too. If what you say is true, and this boy *can* actually see things, then the tradeoff he got sure doesn't sound like it's worth it. You're sure he's okay now?"

She nodded. "At the moment. But I can't stop picturing him on that couch. I'm telling you, Sue, whatever was happening to that boy, it looked like the life was being sucked right out of him."

11

Shannon silently drove north on Verdugo Road and turned her BMW into the IHOP parking lot. She found a space near the front and parked, leaving the car facing the restaurant's entrance.

She turned the ignition off and faced Evan in the passenger seat. "You're sure you're okay?"

He nodded. "I'm fine."

Even though he'd slept for over two hours and looked fine, she was worried he still wasn't being completely open with her. "Listen," she said, stopping him as he reached for the door handle. "I have something I need to talk to you about." She was nervous and could feel her heartbeat increasing. She'd gone over this conversation multiple times in her head but still couldn't seem to find the right words.

Evan turned to her expectantly.

Shannon took a deep breath. "Actually there's something I need to tell you." She realized that she was squeezing the steering wheel and forced herself to let go. "Evan, I haven't been entirely . . . candid with you." She glanced at him nervously, but his face was expressionless. "You have to understand, I want to help you. I really do.

But there's another reason I've become so interested in these episodes of yours—a personal reason."

Evan's face finally began to change, taking on a look of curiosity.

She felt the nervousness in her hands, and swallowed hard. "Evan, something happened to me and my family . . . to my daughter." Shannon hesitated, trying to hold her chin still as she felt it began to quiver. "She was taken."

She hadn't said the words in over a year and found that still, after all this time, she had to force her mouth to say them. "My daughter was kidnapped. She was seven."

Even a year later, nothing had changed. The pain was still there, along with the dread and the horror of it all. Shannon could feel the tears forming in her eyes yet again. She couldn't stop it. "We never . . . we *haven't* found her. She's been gone for a long time, and we still haven't found her."

Evan was stunned. It was the last thing he had expected to hear. He sat in his seat dumbfounded. Finally, he blinked. "How long ago?"

"Eighteen months."

A jolt of recognition hit Evan. Wait, he remembered the news broadcasts on the local stations. He didn't remember Dr. Mayer, but he remembered pictures of her daughter, young with dark hair and green eyes. He had no idea it had been Dr. Mayer's daughter. He looked absentmindedly at the console in front of them, speechless.

Shannon closed her eyes briefly, which sent two tears rolling down her cheeks. "I'm sorry, Evan, I didn't mean to involve you. I didn't mean to let you get hurt." She wiped the tears away and glanced at him. He was still staring straight ahead. "When you told me you saw Tania eating her sandwich that day, I didn't believe it. It was impossible. It had to be. My training told me it was a coincidence, a trick, something I was missing. But at the same time, something deep inside wanted to believe that maybe what you were seeing was real. I secretly began to wish that it was somehow possible. That you could see those things, and if you could, then maybe, just maybe, you could see something else too."

She shook her head again, ashamed. "Deep down I wished for it. I wished for it so badly that I let myself put you in harm's way to find out. I'm sorry, Evan. I'm so sorry. I crossed the line. What you saw today was a terrible mistake. It was a terrible decision, because I wasn't your doctor today. I was a mother. A mother who desperately wants to find out what happened to her daughter."

Evan was watching her with a saddened look on his face. "You don't have to be sorry."

Shannon sniffed and nodded. "Yes, I do need to be sorry. I helped you recreate these episodes, Evan, without even knowing if they were safe. Maybe without even *wanting* to know, and it was all for me. But it should have been about you."

Evan shrugged innocently. "It's okay."

"No, it's not okay," she snapped. "Not as a doctor, not even as a mother. I had no right to do that to you." Shannon wiped her eyes again and turned away. She used him. She used a kid.

Neither of them spoke for a long time until Evan finally broke the silence. "There's something that I haven't told you either," he said quietly.

"What's that?"

Evan lowered his gaze and peered at the dark carpet under his feet. "You asked if I'd seen anything else, other than what we talked about. I lied and said I hadn't. But the truth is I've been seeing a lot of things. And a couple of those times, I saw *you*."

Shannon was surprised. "Me?"

Evan nodded.

"When did you see me?"

"A couple times at night. I didn't mean to; it just happened." He frowned. "You were sitting alone at a table in a dark room, crying. I think you were eating dinner."

"By myself?"

"Uh huh."

She took a deep breath. "Did you see anything else?"

"No," he looked back at her, embarrassed. "I'm sorry, I wanted to tell you but . . . I just, you know."

"It's okay." Shannon blinked several more tears away and thought about what he'd said. "Evan, what exactly do you see when these episodes happen? I mean, what's it like?"

He thought a moment, imagining how to describe it. "It's like a fog, I guess . . . a wall of white fog. I can't see through it, but if I stare at it long enough it starts to clear, kind of like a tunnel that opens. Sometimes I can see through to the other side."

Shannon turned to him. "Do *you* think this is real, Evan?"

"I think so," he replied, with his head still down.

"Evan, I have to be honest with you. I've been a psychiatrist for a long time, and I've helped a lot of people. But I'm not sure I know how to help you with this. In fact, I'm not so sure I even know where to begin."

"Maybe we shouldn't fix it, yet."

Her face showed surprise. *What did he just say?*

Evan didn't continue immediately. Instead, he turned and peered through the front windows of the restaurant. He could see his mother working inside, wearing a light pink uniform. It looked like she had just taken someone's order and was walking back to the counter. He thought of how hard his mother worked for him, how much she gave and how much she gave up so that he could go to a good school, have clothes, and have food. And it wasn't just him; she was always helping people.

Evan watched his mother for a long time before he turned back to Shannon, who was still looking at him with a puzzled expression. "I don't want to try to fix the problem yet, Dr. Mayer. I want to try to help you."

Shannon was shocked. She stared at Evan with her mouth slightly open, but said nothing for a long time.

"Evan . . . I can't even begin to tell you what that means to me. And let me tell you, you're a pretty amazing kid, but I can't let you do that."

"Why?" he asked, confused.

"Evan, what happened to you in my office today was . . . alarming. And that's putting it mildly. I don't know what happens to your body during these episodes, but it nearly scared me and my sister to death. It's very strange and very frightening." She cocked her head, curiously. "Did you actually feel any of it?"

Evan shook his head. "I don't think I felt the things you saw. Inside it kinda feels like . . . an emptiness. Like a hole, right here." He touched his chest lightly. "It doesn't feel like pain . . . it feels like *fear*."

"Fear?"

"Mostly."

Shannon studied him. "Why do you think you're experiencing fear?"

"I'm not sure." He thought about the question. "Maybe because I don't think it's really fog that I'm seeing."

"What do you think it is?"

"I don't know. Something else, something worse."

Shannon put her hand lightly on his arm. "This is exactly what I mean, Evan. Whatever this is, I think it's dangerous, and I can't risk something like that happening to you again. Not because of me."

"I'll be all right."

"Evan, are you listening to yourself?" she asked, incredulously. "You didn't see what happened to your body back there in my office. I did. It was *really* scary, believe me."

He kept his gaze down, contemplating, before finally accepting her answer with a sigh. "Okay." After an uncomfortable silence, he reached for the handle and opened the door, pushing it outward. "Thank you for the ride, Dr. Mayer."

She watched him as he stood up. "Are you *sure* you're okay?"

He glanced back down and gave her a quick grin. "I'm sure." With that, he pushed the car door closed.

Evan walked to the entrance of the restaurant before turning around to watch her drive away. His gaze followed her car all the way back out to Verdugo Road. He still couldn't believe it was Dr. Mayer's daughter who was kidnapped. When the BMW disappeared from sight, Evan turned toward the glass door, accidentally brushing his pants with his right hand. He felt something in his pocket. Curious, he reached in and pulled the object out. It was the quarter the little girl had given him.

12

Shannon barely made it to the end of her driveway, and put the car in park before completely breaking down. She dropped her forehead on the top of the steering wheel and sobbed.

What on earth was she supposed to do? She missed Ellie so much. She wanted so badly to find her. So badly that now she had risked Evan's life. She felt like an awful person, yet all she wanted was her Ellie back. What was she supposed to do, give up? *What if this thing with Evan was real?*

There were a thousand what-ifs, none of them any more likely than the next. Was this what she was mentally and emotionally reduced to, believing in any possibility no matter how bizarre or how hopeless? *God, why not just believe in magic?*

She sat crying in her car for a long time. After what felt like hours, she slowly leaned back against the headrest with tears still streaming down her face. The pain never stopped. *Why her? What horrible thing had she done to deserve this? What had Ellie done?*

Eventually she wiped the tears away with the back of her hand. She looked out over the empty, manicured lawn wondering why she even bothered. *Who cared about the lawn, or the hedge, or the paint on the side of the house for that matter?* In the beginning, she had it maintained because it would be one of the first things Ellie saw when she came home, but after that hope faded she kept the gardeners on just to maintain some stability in her life. Now, a year and a half later, even that didn't matter. *Who cared about any of it?*

She opened her car door and stepped out onto the driveway's smooth concrete. She tucked her purse under her arm and gently pushed the door shut behind her. Shannon stood staring at the house, feeling the sense of dread fill her body again. She hated coming home. It felt like living in a graveyard.

Once inside, she closed the oversized front door and walked down the short, darkened hallway. As she walked, the clicking from her heels echoed off the wooden floor. The kitchen looked immaculate, with nothing out of place, but upon closer inspection it was evident most of the items had not been used in a very long time.

Shannon dropped her purse onto the counter and stood still, listening. With a heavy sigh, she walked back toward the door and began climbing the stairs.

——•——

Dennis Mayer didn't hear his wife approach from down the hall, nor did he hear her open the door. He sat in a small chair, staring out the window as the sun began its afternoon descent. Outside, the trees swayed gently in the breeze.

Shannon peered from the doorway and watched her husband as he sat, consumed by their loss. It was the worst possible thing a parent could ever imagine, and it had hit him devastatingly hard.

She finally cleared her throat. "Are you hungry?" He didn't answer. "Dennis?"

With a jolt of surprise, he turned his head. "What?"

"Are you hungry?"

He seemed to think about the question as if he'd never heard it before. "No," he answered, turning back to the window.

Behind him, Shannon rolled her eyes as they began tearing up again. *Was it ever going to stop?* She opened her mouth to reply but stopped herself. She left the door open, and headed back to the stairs.

Dennis Mayer was caught in the trap of a depression as deep as any his wife had witnessed. He now sat in the chair all day, every day, gently rocking the glider back and forth with an expressionless stare. He used to wear his uniform and stand while looking out the window, but not anymore. Now he barely bothered to dress at all. Instead, he just sat . . . and rocked.

They'd kept Ellie's room exactly as it was the day she'd disappeared. The only change they made was to make the bed and return her stuffed animals to their place on the pillows. Everything else was the same, and it was where Detective Dennis Mayer felt the closest to her. The dresser, the clothes in the closet, even the crayons strewn on the floor, all made him feel as though she were somehow there, with him.

Even the glider chair he sat in was hers. It was her favorite place to sit and read during rainy days. It was where she was nursed as a baby. That room was all he had left to cling to.

He used to sit in the room to think, hoping that something, anything, would stir a memory or a thought and provide a clue to give him a new place to look. After taking leave from the LAPD, he had spent every minute of every day looking. He studied every possible clue, every piece of paper, every word from every eyewitness. Something must have been left; someone must have seen something significant, even if they didn't know it. He talked to the same eyewitnesses over and over until they finally stopped calling him back, or refused to answer the door.

That's when he had his epiphany. *He shouldn't be focused on who saw Ellie's abduction, he should be focused on who took her!* He was a cop for Christ's sake. He'd put so many people in jail it wasn't even funny; people who had every reason, and more than enough time, to dream of their revenge.

It took almost a year to track down every convict, every defendant, every arrest, every single person who might have thought he'd wronged them. And he memorized every word of their cases. But he found nothing. The only possible exception had been a slimy ex-principal that Dennis and his partner had busted and helped put in prison for twelve years. A bad economy and an overburdened state prison system sent that one home on early release, but nothing ever indicated he was involved in Ellie's disappearance, not a single clue. And God knows Dennis looked. He'd even broken into the man's apartment in a desperate attempt to dig something up, but eventually he had to admit he'd hit a dead end.

With each passing month, his desperation slowly turned into depression as Dennis ran out of ideas about where else to look. He had racked his brain endlessly and come up empty.

Whoever wanted revenge on him was smarter than he was. They had stolen his little girl from him and over time turned him into a shell of a man. The most fundamental role of a father was to protect his children, to protect his family. And Dennis Mayer had failed miserably. That guilt alone would have been enough, but it was *how* Ellie was taken that truly destroyed him.

He was the one who was supposed to pick Ellie up from school that day. His wife had reminded him twice that morning, but later, after getting caught up in a significant break they received in a case, he did the unthinkable . . . he forgot. He forgot to get his little girl on time. And in the forty-five minutes she sat in front of the school, wondering and waiting for her daddy, she disappeared.

He was a complete failure, both as a husband and a father.

13

From the outside, the Glendale Central Library on Harvard Street looked more like an office building than a library. But its beautifully renovated interior, and familiar smell of old books, more than made up for that. Evan's archaic home computer was having problems, which meant a fifteen-minute trip downtown to use one of the library's machines. Sitting at the new, modern desk, it didn't take long to find what he was looking for, and once he did, he read from the screen very carefully.

According to the newspaper archive, seven-year-old Elizabeth Mayer was kidnapped near her elementary school at approximately 12:30 p.m., on one of the busiest school days of that year. The entire school had gotten out at once, due to one of the district's mandatory teacher conference days.

A few kids had reported seeing Ellie walking down the street, and one classmate thought he even saw her get into a car, but couldn't remember what the car looked like. When it was discovered that she was the daughter of a local police officer, every off-duty cop in the city showed up within minutes to help. The newspaper article described the entire city as being in a veritable lockdown. Nearby neighborhoods were searched, and drivers on most major roads were stopped and questioned. A local Amber Alert was issued in record time, resulting in hundreds of possible leads, which quickly poured in from as far away as Anaheim. But in the end, none of them led to anything tangible, nor were the police able to turn up any solid clues from the scene. Even after studying video from the traffic cameras, and a couple of pictures taken by parents in the area at that time, the case of Ellie Mayer faded into obscurity and was categorized as "unsolved."

Evan stared at one of the "missing" pictures of Ellie with her hair pulled back in a ponytail and a wide smile on her face. He remembered her clearly now from the news broadcasts.

He leaned back in his chair, still staring at the screen. She was a beautiful little girl; the look on her face was so happy and so innocent. He was only eighteen, and he could not begin to imagine what Dr. Mayer had suffered through, what she was still suffering through, but he understood its depth. And he puzzled over her resolve in saying that she didn't want him to help.

He crossed his arms, hooking one hand into the crook of each elbow. He didn't even know if he could help. Something strange was happening to him, something dangerous, but if there was even a chance of finding out what happened to her . . . shouldn't he at least try?

Evan knew Dr. Mayer was worried about what might happen to him, and as bad as that was, he still hadn't told her about the other effect of his episodes. Something that was far more frightening to him. He sure couldn't tell her now.

—•—

Tania knocked gently on the large office door and poked her head in.

"Excuse me, Dr. Mayer?"

Shannon brought her face up from her hands and blinked hard. "Yes, what is it?"

"I know you told me to cancel all of your appointments today, but Evan Nash wants to talk to you."

Shannon blinked again with a confused expression. She glanced down at her phone but didn't see any lights flashing. "Is he on the phone?" she asked.

"No." Tania tilted her head. "He's here in front, at my desk."

"He's here?" Shannon's eyes widened. "Did he say what for?"

"No, should I bring him back?"

"Yes, yes, please." Shannon sat up and instinctively began straightening things on her desk. She picked up a pen before catching herself. She studied the pen for a moment and set it down calmly.

A few moments later, Tania quietly opened the door again. "Here you go, Evan."

"Thanks." He smiled at Tania with a touch of nervousness, and squeezed past her into the room.

Shannon took a deep breath and came around her desk. "Hello Evan, this is a surprise. What can I do for you?"

Evan glanced at the door as it clicked shut, then he turned back to her. "I went to the library yesterday, and I've been doing some thinking." He paused, waiting for Dr. Mayer to respond as she normally would, with a question. He chuckled to himself but didn't let it show. He took a deep breath. "I don't know what this 'thing' is, but I want to help you try to find out about your daughter."

Shannon's eyes showed her sadness. "Evan, we talked about this. We can't. *I can't.* I—"

He cut her off. "Listen! Wait. I know you think this is dangerous, but I can handle it. I promise."

She frowned.

"I mean it," he pressed.

Shannon didn't move. She kept her stoic gaze on the boy. "Evan, we don't even know what it is that's happening to you, let alone how to *handle* it. This could kill you, Evan. Do you understand that? It could *kill* you."

"It won't," he insisted.

"How do you know that? How do you know? Because from what I saw two days ago, it damn near did!"

"I just want to help."

"Why Evan? Why risk it?"

Evan stood his ground. He swallowed hard, and lowered his head. "I had a sister who died when I was little," he said softly. "She was four. I was six."

Shannon was frozen. She didn't know what to say.

He nervously pushed his hands into his pockets. "Her name was Elizabeth. I still think about her. Sometimes I wonder if she would be proud of her big brother."

Shannon placed her hand on her chest. She could see his pain. "Do you want to talk a little bit about it?"

He shook his head. "No."

"Okay."

"Dr. Mayer, I know you don't want to," Evan said, raising his head. "But you have to let me try to help."

Shannon rolled her eyes and turned away. *Don't want to? Don't want to?* Jesus, she was on the verge of losing her mind. He couldn't possibly know that she was hanging on by a thread, barely making it from day to day. She could feel herself slipping into that dark, horrible place that had already claimed her husband. *Then what . . . who would search for Ellie then?* She looked at the ceiling, and felt the tears begin to return. She had to do something. She had to! Because there was something she hadn't told anyone, something even worse. She was running out of time.

———•———

Less than a mile away, Mary Creece winked at her elderly patient and gently closed the examining room door. She slid the thick chart into the plastic holder mounted outside of the door and glanced down as her phone buzzed. She reached into her pocket and pulled it out, examining the number displayed.

She ducked into an empty room and accepted the call. "Hi Sue."

"Mary, I think I have something on our boy Evan."

"Really? That was fast. It's only been two days."

"What can I tell you," Sue Bales replied. "I work fast. Besides, most journals and archive records are computerized these days, although in this case that wasn't a lot of help."

"Did you find something?"

"I did. But I didn't find it in any database, at least not one of my medical databases. It actually turned up in a very unlikely place, Google Books."

Mary was surprised. "All you had to do was Google?"

"Not exactly. I'm referring to the Google project. They've spent the last several years scanning and digitizing the contents of old books that were published before computers and before digital copies. They've got teams all over the country, sitting in libraries with nothing more than a laptop and a scanner."

Mary turned and peered out the second-story window as she spoke. "What does that have to do with Evan?"

"It has to do with him because I couldn't find anything resembling his pattern of symptoms in any of my usual databases. What I did find turned up in an old book that Google had scanned into the system. Anyway, this book mentions an article submitted to the *Annals of Family Care*, a very small and obscure journal that went out of business in 1985, and it also describes some symptoms . . . symptoms that sound eerily familiar."

Mary took a breath, excited. She reached out and gently closed the door. "So what exactly did you find?"

"It's too much to tell you on the phone. But it's not good. Where are you now?"

"I'm at work."

"What's the address?"

"295 Cypress, suite 210."

"Good. I'm coming to you," Sue said.

———•———

Evan positioned himself on the couch and adjusted his body, trying to get comfortable. He closed his eyes for a moment, following the sound of Dr. Mayer moving from window to window, closing each of the room's shades. With less light, the cherrywood furniture and leather upholstery appeared even darker. A few moments later, she returned to her chair beside him.

She sighed and looked softly at him. "Remember, I'm going to wake you up at the first sign of stress."

"Okay," he agreed.

Shannon slipped the pulse oximeter over his fingertip and turned on the small machine that her sister had left behind. She placed a strip on his forehead and ran her finger gently over it, pressing the simple thermometer in place.

"Are you ready?"

"Yes."

Shannon swiveled around in the chair and grabbed her purse. Reaching inside, she retrieved her wallet and proceeded to pull out several photos. She placed the wallet on her desk and spun back to Evan. "Here are the most recent ones I have."

Evan took the pictures, six in all, and studied them. They were pictures of her daughter Ellie; two looked like class pictures, another showed her kneeling with a soccer ball, and the rest were family photos from various occasions. He focused on each one for a long time, trying to memorize them.

He'd *seen* people before when he pictured them in his head. He prayed he could do the same thing again, but this time intentionally. More importantly, he prayed he could do it quickly, before the *fear* came.

Evan placed the photos on his chest and closed his blue-gray eyes. He calmed his breathing and felt his heartbeat begin to slow. One by one, he let each muscle in his body relax and waited for the weariness to take him.

It took longer this time, but almost ten minutes later, Shannon watched him finally let go, and saw his head roll slightly to the side. The electronic monitor continued to beep methodically, with both pulse and oxygen levels normal. She looked at the pictures on his chest and then she turned her eyes back to his face. Her heart was racing faster than his. *Please God.*

The seconds ticked by unmercifully as Shannon glanced back and forth between Evan's body and the monitor. But before two minutes had passed, it happened.

The beeping frequency increased without warning, and his temperature began to change. She pumped the cuff on his arm and measured his blood pressure. It was coming down fast!

Shannon touched the skin on his arm and gasped. His temperature wasn't just falling; it was plummeting, and so fast that she could feel him grow colder!

She grabbed Evan and shook him hard, but got no response. She shook again, harder. "Evan!" she yelled. *"Evan!"*

She twisted her hands into his shirt and shook him back and forth as hard as she could. *"Evan!"* Her eyes bulged. *He's not waking up!* The lights on the monitor suddenly started flashing red.

Without a second thought, she reeled back and slapped him across the face, hard enough to make his head turn to the other side. *"Evaan!"*

Nothing. Frantically, she hit him again, and watched in horror as the color appeared to drain from his face.

—•—

Outside, Tania nearly jumped out of her chair when Shannon came screaming out of her office, *"TANIA, CALL 911 NOW!"*

14

The urgent care waiting room at Glendale General Hospital was unusually quiet when Connie Nash came through the doors. Shannon had only met her once, during the first visit with Evan, but she recognized his mother immediately. And it was the moment she was dreading since making the call.

"How is he?" Connie cried.

Shannon held up her hands nervously as Connie Nash approached. "I don't know yet. The doctor hasn't come out."

"What in God's name happened?"

Shannon swallowed. "He had a reaction in my office. His body had a powerful physiological response during one of his episodes, a bad one."

Connie stared at her incredulously. "How bad?"

"Bad enough to be in ICU."

"Oh my God!" His mother gasped. "What happened to my baby?" She was unable to say more. Shannon closed the distance between them and put her hand on the woman's arm. "He did get here with a pulse, which is critical. So he stands a good chance—"

"A chance?" Connie cut her off. "A chance? He only has a *chance!*" She began to cry. "I don't understand. He was getting help. How could this happen?"

Shannon wanted to tell her the truth but she couldn't. Not there, not yet.

"Ms. Nash," she said, helping her down into a chair. "Evan's problem is more severe than I thought, but I promise you, when he gets out of here, we're going to fix this for good."

Connie looked up at Shannon, who could see the woman was in mild shock. "I can't . . . I don't . . ." She peered up at Shannon helplessly, then let her face fall back down into her hands. "My God, he's all I have in this world. *He's all I have.*"

"He's going to be fine," Shannon whispered. She had no idea if this was true.

—•—

Less than five minutes later, the large white door opened and a doctor in light-blue scrubs emerged. He spotted the women and walked briskly over to them. As he approached, he removed his cap and crumpled it in his hands.

"Ms. Nash?" he asked, looking to the older of the two.

"Is he okay?" she asked urgently, standing up. They both held their breath.

The doctor frowned. "I wouldn't describe it as *okay*, but he is stronger than when he got here, which is promising. Unfortunately, he's still unconscious, and we can't seem to bring him out of it without some aggressive medical intervention, which we'd rather not do."

"My baby." His mother moaned. Shannon saw her begin to slump, as if she might faint, and quickly put a supportive hand under the woman's arm. "What does that mean?"

"Now, please understand," the doctor held up his hand in a cautionary gesture, "that even though we can't revive him at the moment, he's also not showing signs of internal trauma, which could indicate something more akin to a coma. So that's the good news."

Connie placed her hand on her chest and took a breath. "And what's the bad news?"

"Well," he said delicately, "the bad news is that without aggressive treatment, the alternative is to simply wait this out."

Shannon folded her arms across her chest. "So is there anything else wrong, physically?"

The doctor raised a brow and shook his head. "No. As a matter of fact, his vital signs are stable, so we have some reason to be optimistic."

"Can I see him?" Connie asked.

"Yes, of course, just give us a few minutes to finish some tests and one of the nurses will bring you in."

She frowned, but accepted his answer. The doctor shook both their hands and headed back through the large door.

The women turned to face one another again when someone called out from behind them.

"Shannon!"

They turned to find Mary running toward them, with her friend Sue Bales following quickly behind. They reached the two women a little out of breath.

"How is he?"

"He's improving." Shannon glanced at Evan's mother then looked back to both Mary and Sue. "We're . . . optimistic. Mary, this is Connie Nash, Evan's mother."

"It's very nice to meet you," Mary said, shaking her hand. Sue reached around her friend and did the same. After a long moment, Mary turned to her sister.

"Shannon, can we speak to you for a moment?"

"Sure," she replied. She apologized to Connie and excused herself, following the two women back down the hall and out of earshot. Mary noticed a small private room with a sign on the door that read "Counseling." She peeked inside to find it empty, stepped in, and held the door open for the other two.

When the door closed, Mary almost screamed at her sister. *"What the hell did you do?"*

Shannon jumped and looked at both women with a helpless expression. "He, he wanted to try again."

Mary stared at her aghast, trying to comprehend her sister's actions. "He wanted to do it again, so you said *yes?*"

"Wait, wait," Shannon stopped and closed her eyes, trying to calm the stuttering. "Listen, I didn't have a choice. He came to my office, wanting to try it again. He wanted to help."

"Who the hell cares what he wanted!" cried Mary. "This is dangerous and you knew it. You should have told him no!"

Shannon shot back: "Listen to me! I couldn't . . . just say no." She stopped and stared hard at her sister. She took a deep breath. "He was going to do it anyway." Shannon briefly eyed her sister's friend, then looked back to Mary. "He told me he wanted to try to help. He'd do it at home if he had to. What was I supposed to do, let him do it again completely unsupervised? He thought he could control it this time, but he couldn't. Obviously. But if he had done it at home, he probably wouldn't even have made it here!"

"You could have talked him out of it."

"No, I couldn't have. I tried. But he was convinced he would be all right."

"Then you could have at least called me."

Shannon's eyes widened in anger. "I tried! I got your voice mail."

Mary didn't answer. Instead she stood steadfast with crossed arms, glaring at her sister.

Sue, who had remained quiet during their exchange, cleared her throat. "So what did the doctor really say?"

Mary finally dropped her hands and placed them on her hips, still glaring at Shannon. "You remember my friend Sue."

"Yes." Shannon nodded, and turned to face her. "He told Evan's mother that it wasn't a coma, and she should be optimistic. But the real message was that they have no idea what's wrong. And they can't wake him up." Shannon dropped her head. The message wasn't lost on anyone in the room. A thought suddenly came to her and she looked back to Mary. "What are you doing here anyway?"

"Looking for you. We called your office, and Tania told us what happened, so we came straight here."

Shannon thought for a moment, and backed up, sitting down on the edge of a small, round table. "Why were you looking for me?"

Mary frowned, and looked at Sue. "Show her."

Sue stepped forward and slid a large leather satchel off her shoulder. She turned it sideways and plopped it onto the table next to Shannon. "Your sister came to see me after the episode at your office on Saturday. I'm not sure if you know, but I head up a medical research team at my company."

"I remember." Shannon nodded.

"Mary gave me the details of what happened and asked if I could help try to track down any records of similar cases. Well, I found one," she said, and reached into the satchel, pulling out a tall, leather-bound book. "In the early 1990s, a medical student writing her dissertation cited a little-known medical journal. She specifically referenced an article submitted by a family doctor in Montana in 1982." Sue unwound a small string from the front of the leather book. "In the journal entry, the doctor describes a patient who began experiencing very strange symptoms after a driving accident. The patient was twenty-three years old and not only experienced the exact same problems, but also started having *visions*."

Shannon gasped. "Visions, like Evan's?"

"Yes." Sue opened the book and turned it to a page she had marked. "The company that published this journal went out of business just a few years after the article was published. It took me almost two days to find a copy of it. Fortunately, I have a friend in San Diego who is even more obsessed with this stuff than I am." She turned the book toward Shannon and pointed to the text near the bottom of the left-hand page.

Shannon leaned over the book, reading. There wasn't much more detail than what Sue had already mentioned. "It doesn't list the patient's name, just the doctor."

"The journal doesn't list the patient's name," replied Sue, "but the medical student's dissertation did. The name is Dan Taylor. I don't know how that girl found it, but she did."

Shannon read the short paragraphs three times before straightening back up. "Butte, Montana?"

"Butte, Montana." Mary nodded.

Shannon looked at her sister and then to Sue. "So where is Dan Taylor now?"

"He's dead."

Shannon was stunned, and stared blankly down at the open journal.

Behind her, Mary approached and placed her hand quietly on her sister's shoulder.

"What did he die of?" whispered Shannon.

"This." Mary lowered her voice. "Whatever is happening to Evan was happening to him too, and it eventually killed him."

Without a word, Sue slid a piece of paper across the table. It was a photocopy of the death certificate.

Shannon looked at it for a long time. "My God, what have I done?"

Mary sighed, and put both hands on her sister's shoulders. "Listen, Shannon, I'm sorry for what I said. It's not your fault." She could see the tears in her sister's eyes. "If he was going to do it, then he was going to do it. You couldn't have stopped that. And you're right . . . at least you were able to get him here quickly."

Shannon didn't reply. She stared at the death certificate on the table, motionless. Very slowly, she reached down and picked up the photocopy. *Was there going to be another one just like it with Evan's name?* "There's another reason," she said, and covered her eyes with the palms of her hands. "There's another reason I helped him again."

Mary and Sue exchanged puzzled looks. "What do you mean?"

"Evan said he would do it himself if he had to, it's true," she sniffed. "But there's something else I haven't told you." She rolled her eyes toward the ceiling. "I've been having a . . . *feeling*. A feeling that something is about to go wrong, really wrong. It's been absolute torture this whole time without Ellie, eighteen months of pain and despair so deep that most of the time I just want to curl up and die. And yet now I'm feeling something even worse."

Mary reached out and took her hand. "What is it, Sis?"

"I don't know," Shannon answered, as tears streaked down her face. "I don't know what it is or what it means. I just feel like something horrible is about to happen, more horrible than everything else." She wrapped her arms around Mary. "I helped Evan today, even after last time, knowing it was dangerous. I did it because whatever this feeling is, it feels like I'm running out of time."

"Out of time for what?" Mary asked.

Shannon raised her head from her sister's shoulder. "I don't know. I just don't know."

"What did you just say?"

All three women whirled around in response to the loud voice behind them. It was Evan's mother standing in the open doorway with her hand on the doorknob.

Shannon gasped.

"What the hell did you just say?" Connie Nash demanded. "Did you just say you did this to my son *again*, already knowing he was in danger?"

The three women stared at her in shock. Shannon's and Mary's expressions quickly changed to guilt.

"M-Ms. Nash," Shannon stammered. "How long . . ."

"I've been standing here longer than you think! Tell me I heard you wrong," she screamed. *"Tell me!"*

Their mouths hung open, as they tried to think of what to say. But Shannon knew there was no backtracking. God, why hadn't she turned around and locked the door?

Connie Nash was seething. "You put my son in this hospital and now he is fighting for his life! All to serve yourself! I trusted you. I knew who you were when we came to you, and I still trusted you. My God, I actually felt bad for you, and now you've sacrificed my son!"

She abruptly took a step toward them, which made the other women move backward. "Tell me I'm wrong!" she yelled again. "Can you? *Can you?*" Her voice was icy. "I'm calling my lawyer, and I swear to God I will see you in jail!"

15

Shannon looked upward, at the huge glass arch over the front entrance of the hospital. Mary and Sue stood behind her. This was all she needed. She was already struggling with so much; now Evan was in the ICU, and his mother wanted to put her behind bars. She felt like she was suffocating. *What else could possibly go wrong?*

Shannon turned and wearily faced the other two. "Now what?"

"Sis," said Mary, "you need to go home and rest."

Shannon shrugged. "I think I should call my attorney."

"Fine, but then go home. Even if she's serious about a lawsuit, it's going to take some time. Right now, you need rest."

"What are you going to do?"

Mary glanced back to Sue, who gave her a nod of support. "We're going to the airport."

"What! Why?"

"We're going to Montana, to find that doctor."

16

The CRJ-701 airliner lowered its landing gear and banked to the left as it continued down through its descent. Even from some altitude, there was just enough light on the horizon to see the large patches of snow on the ground below.

Mary looked out across the small city of Butte, Montana, once named the Richest Hill on Earth after the copper mining boom created by the advent of electricity in the late nineteenth century. That electricity now powered the streetlights stretching throughout the small town, giving off a warm, golden glow as stars began to dot the dark-blue sky above. A rising crescent moon hovered atop the mountains far in the distance.

She leaned back from the window and watched as Sue powered down her laptop computer and slid it into her bag. Both women were anxious to land and check on Evan's condition, not having had time during the rush for their connecting flight in Billings. They were praying for good news.

They also knew it was going to be a long night. The County Recorder's office would not be open until 9 a.m. the following morning. Sue hadn't found a death certificate for Dr. Jim Rief, the doctor who originally submitted the strange medical case, and they were hopeful he was still alive. But the doctor had long since retired, and there was no record of a home address for him. To make matters worse, according to satellite pictures, his office had been bulldozed long ago. Their first priority was to find out what happened to the doctor and what he might know about Evan's malady. They prayed he would know something that could help Evan before it was too late.

The bounce onto the runway shook the passengers from side to side, and the plane began to slow. After a brief taxi to a tiny terminal, both women stood up, grabbed their bags, and awkwardly shuffled down the aisle with the rest of the passengers. As they stepped from the plane and into the Jetway, both felt a momentary chill of cold air seeping in from the outside. They quickly made their way up the ramp, where Mary pulled out her cell phone to call the hospital.

A few minutes later her heart sank. She ended the call, dropping the phone back into her purse. "No change."

"At all?" Sue asked.

"No. He's still unconscious and his vitals are the same."

Sue grabbed her bag and kept walking. "Then let's hurry."

———•———

The motel was just a few minutes away. After opening the door to their room, Sue set up her laptop. Once she got an Internet connection, Sue opened a browser window and started typing, while Mary watched.

"I had a thought on the plane," Sue said. "Trying to verify the doctor's status by searching through the death certificates may take too long, especially since we can't get in until tomorrow. I may have a better idea." She typed an address and waited for the page to load. "It may be faster to trace the ownership of the physical address. If we can find out who the owner of the lot was in the early 1980s, we may be able to find them and ask if they know what happened to the doctor. At the very least, we might glean some personal information from records or applications from Rief. Even an old home address would give us a place to start."

"I'm getting the feeling this could take a long time."

Sue stopped her typing for a moment. "It might. Small towns don't usually have the most accurate records, but Butte has a lot of theirs digitized. I noticed they partner with a software company to maintain their archive data. That could really help us, assuming the outfit is archiving things like business licenses, and not just birth and death certificates." Sue typed in the ID and password she had created earlier for this site, and waited for a list of records to display.

Mary bent down and peered over her shoulder. "Well, at least it's a small town. People tend to know each other."

"Right." Sue navigated to the County Assessor's page and clicked the Real Estate Parcel option. She took a small notebook from her purse, where she had written the address of the old lot, and she typed that into the blank on the screen. The site took several moments to search, but eventually displayed the ownership history of the parcel, highlighted in yellow. It appeared the same person had owned it for most of the 1980s.

"The owner's name was Evelyn Sutton," Sue said, pulling her phone out of her purse. "And it has an address and phone number. They're old, but it's a place to start."

"Give me the number for the hospital," Mary said as she stood up. "Maybe I can track down Dr. Rief from another direction."

Sue looked up the hospital's phone number, wrote it on a piece of paper, and handed it to Mary. She turned her attention back to the property owner and dialed her number.

Mary walked to the other side of the room and dialed the hospital on her own phone. The main number didn't pick up but the recording referred her to the emergency room for after-hours assistance. When she dialed that number, a woman's voice answered.

"Hello," Mary said. "I have a strange question for you. I'm trying to find a doctor that worked in town a long time ago and am wondering if you have any records indicating where I might find him."

"What's his name?" the nurse asked on the other end.

"James Rief. I believe he had a small practice in town in the '80s, off of Harrison."

"Who's calling?"

"My name is Mary Creece. I'm a nurse in Los Angeles. I'm trying to find Dr. Rief regarding a patient we may have in common."

"In common" was a bit of a stretch, Mary thought, but she knew most hospitals these days were leery about divulging information, especially to strangers over the phone.

"Mmm," said the other voice. "And who are you again?"

Mary could sense the woman hesitating. She needed to act quickly before the woman simply put up a wall of hospital procedure. "I'm Mary," she said, softening her voice. "I'm sorry to bother you. I know it's a pain when people call me for this stuff. I never thought I would be the one on the other end." She feigned a friendly laugh, and could hear the other woman chuckle in response. "It's just that I've got this sick kid, and I think Dr. Rief may have some experience with whatever this is."

"I see," the woman replied. "Unfortunately, I don't have access to any of the older records at this hour. We're pretty much the only part of the hospital open right now. Is this urgent?"

Mary frowned. "Yeah, it kind of is."

"Well," the woman paused to think. "We do have a doctor on call tonight who's a little older and has been around for a while. I can ask him if the name rings a bell, but unfortunately I can't look up anything that far back for you until the records office opens in the morning."

"That would be great, thank you. If you could please ask the doctor, I would appreciate it. Can I give you my number?"

Mary gave the nurse her cell number, thanked her again, and hung up. She was not all that surprised. In small towns most things were closed in the evenings. Maybe she would get lucky with the on-call doctor, but if not she'd try again in the morning. This time in person. She turned to Sue, who had just hung up her own phone.

"That was Evelyn Sutton's son. His mother is rather old, but he said we could come over and talk to her if we can make it there before nine." She glanced at her watch. "That gives us twenty minutes for a thirty-minute drive."

———•———

They made it, thanks to Sue's long-standing aversion to speed limits, but in the end Evelyn Sutton had no idea where Dr. Rief might be living. It had been almost twenty years since she'd seen him. She did, however, invite the women to go through some of her old records in the attic. She had managed several properties during that time but had sold them all off. The plot where Rief's office once stood was the last one sold.

Mary and Sue spent an hour going through the two boxes of paper but found nothing. Exasperated, they thanked the Suttons and saw their way to the door.

When they reached the car, Sue looked across the hood to Mary. "Did anything strike you as a little odd about that?"

"About what? The old lady?" Mary's breath was easily visible in the cold air.

"No. The boxes of records," Sue said.

"Well, it was a major letdown," Mary said, with a shrug. "We didn't find anything at all. We're no closer than we were."

Sue shook her head and lowered her voice. "Something wasn't right, Mary. Did you notice how clean the woman's house was?

That woman is very detailed, even at her age. I do believe that she couldn't remember anything after all these years, but those boxes were detailed and very organized. As far as I could tell she had records for every renter she'd *ever* had, except one."

"Dr. Rief," Mary whispered.

Sue nodded. "And she was genuinely surprised it was not in there."

"So what happened to it?" Mary pondered.

"That's a good question."

The women stood looking at each other for a long moment, thinking, until they were interrupted by the ringtone from Mary's phone. She looked at the brightly lit screen and shot a look at Sue. "It's the hospital."

She accepted the call and held the phone to her ear. "Hello, this is Mary."

They both climbed back into the warm car while Mary spoke. The call lasted only a few minutes, but at the end, Mary pulled out a pen and paper and wrote down some information. When she hung up, Mary raised an eyebrow at Sue. "That was the on-call doctor. He remembers Dr. Rief. He said they even went fishing together a few times back then, but he hasn't talked to him in many years. He's not sure what happened to him."

Sue sighed and rested her head against the headrest. "Mary, I think we need to prepare ourselves for the possibility that Dr. Rief may be dead."

"Maybe," she answered, thinking. "But there is one more thing. This doctor said that Rief had a small cabin in the mountains, which is where they'd gone fishing. He didn't have the address, but he did tell me how to get there."

"Where?" At that moment Sue's phone chirped. She held it up and peered at the screen as Mary answered her. "About two hours south, but he warned me, it was not an easy drive."

"Hmm."

"What is it?" Mary asked.

Sue finished reading the message on her phone. "I asked one of my team members to help me with the research. He has friends at several of the large phone companies. It seems that the local phone company servicing the Butte area back then was bought out by AT&T a few years ago. Looks like he found a phone record for a Dr. Rief in 1982. The account listed two separate phone numbers with different prefixes."

"That probably means two different locations."

Sue nodded and looked back down at her phone, which was lighting her face in an eerie glow. "One of the phone numbers was disconnected in 1983. That was one year after Rief submitted the case about his patient Dan Taylor to that medical journal."

"It sounds like that's about when he disappeared."

Sue turned and looked back at Mary. "And yet the second number on his account wasn't disconnected for another whole year after that."

"The one with a different prefix?"

"Correct."

"Does your friend know where that other number was located?"

"No," Sue shook her head.

"Maybe the location was the cabin in the mountains."

Sue turned to Mary. "I guess we're about to find out."

17

As much as they hated to do it, the women decided to wait until morning before heading south. They guessed that two hours each way, and through the mountains, might be pushing the range of their rental car's gas tank. And given that they had twenty-year-old directions, there was a good chance of getting lost. The smart thing to do was to wait until daylight to make the search easier. They were both up and in the car by 6 a.m.

Sue eased the car south on Highway 15, while Mary spoke on the phone. When she hung up, her look of concern deepened. "Still no change with Evan."

Sue looked absently to her left at a passing car, the only other one on the road with them. "You realize this is a long shot."

"I know," Mary acknowledged, peering out the front window.

"Well, there's always the County Recorder when we get back." She tried to sound encouraging, but Mary said nothing.

—◆—

It took longer than two hours to locate the small county road they were looking for. It appeared very old, with a surface so rough they felt it was trying to beat their car to death. When it became a dirt road, driving got even worse.

Sue watched the gas gauge carefully as they drove farther and farther in. Once they got down to half a tank they would have to turn back; which, judging from the car's display, would not be long.

Next to her, Mary read her notes again. "I think," she said reluctantly after several minutes, "we should have seen it by now."

Sue grimaced and glanced at the paper.

"He said a small road that connects at a tight angle on the right," Mary repeated. "But I don't see . . ."

She was silenced when Sue slammed on the brakes. They both peered searchingly out the side window at what looked like a small double path, barely big enough for a car. There was an old iron gate in front.

"I don't remember him saying anything about a gate," Mary murmured. "But that is a tight angle. Do you think we should try it?"

Sue looked at her phone. No signal. They were both becoming nervous. Two women in the middle of nowhere, with four sentences of scribbled directions and no way to call for help. In hindsight, this was not looking like their best decision.

They each took a deep breath and reminded one another why they were there. Mary got out and examined the gate. It wasn't locked but it wasn't easy to open either. When it did open, the gate made a terrible groan and shuddered as she pushed it all the way back past the post.

The road, if anyone could call it that, was shrouded by a dense canopy of juniper trees overhead. After a quarter mile of inching slowly down the narrow, bumpy road and dodging mud holes made by nearby melting snow, they spotted the outline of a modest log cabin near the top of a small hill. As they approached, they could see chairs on the porch and curtains in the windows, but no cars.

Sue brought the car to a stop and looked around, her eyes coming back to the cabin. "Think anyone's home?"

"There's only one way to find out."

Both women got out of the car and approached the cabin, the gravel beneath their feet crunching loudly with every step. They reached the wooden steps and climbed up to the large porch. After one more look around, Mary reached forward and knocked on the door's small, glass window.

They froze when they heard the unmistakable slide action of a shotgun behind them.

"Turn around slowly," growled a deep voice.

Instinctively the two women raised their hands in front of them and turned around to face the frightening end of a shotgun barrel. Behind it was the obscured face of someone who looked very dangerous. They remained still, not daring to move any further.

The man kept the barrel pointed at them but said nothing. Instead, he waited, listening. After several long seconds, he took a small step forward. "What are you doing here?"

Neither of the women spoke immediately. They were petrified; the man had his finger on the trigger, and he looked like he was about to pull it.

"W-we're looking for someone," Mary stammered.

"Who?" He demanded.

"A doctor."

The man studied both women. One was shorter with a blonde ponytail and glasses, while the other was a tall, lean woman with red hair and a lighter complexion. Their postures and mannerisms appeared genuine. "Who are you?"

"We're nurses," Mary replied. "From Los Angeles."

"So what the hell are you doing all the way up here, on my property?"

"We're looking for a doctor," Sue repeated. "We're not really sure where he lives. Or lived," she said, correcting herself. When the man didn't answer, she added, "He used to live up here in the '80s."

His eyes narrowed. "You talking about Rief?"

"Yes," Mary said, with a trace of excitement. "Dr. Rief. Do you know where he lives?"

The man shook his head slightly. "He's been gone a long time." He took aim at them again. "Now get the hell out of here."

Mary turned nervously to Sue, then back toward the man at the base of the steps. "D-do you know where we can find him?"

"You can't," he said, his tone a deep growl. "He's dead."

Their fearful expressions were instantly replaced by those of shock.

"Dead? Are you sure?"

"Yes!" he said angrily. "Now get off my porch and off of my property!"

"Okay, okay!" They jumped, keeping their hands raised, and quickly descended the stairs, passing him as he stepped back and followed them with his gun.

As they walked slowly away from the cabin, Sue suddenly stopped and turned around. He was still pointing the shotgun at them but had relaxed a bit. She looked up and curiously followed the roofline of the small house.

"What are you doing?" Mary whispered.

"Look at the roof," she replied, motioning upwards.

Irritated, the man took a few steps forward. "I said leave!"

Sue studied him for several seconds. "Are you sure you don't know where Dr. Rief is?"

"I said he's dead."

Sue tried to stay calm. "I notice you don't have any wires running to your cabin roof. For example, like a *phone line*."

He didn't reply, nor did he follow her gaze up to the roof. Instead, he glared at her.

"You also remembered the doctor's name awfully quickly. I suspect after twenty years most people would've had to stop and think about it." She continued studying the man. "Mary," she finally whispered, "I don't think we're lost."

They watched as the man looked past them and then scanned the area on either side.

Mary whispered back, "Do you think he knows where the doctor is?"

"Actually," Sue replied loud enough for him to hear their conversation. "I think the doctor is standing right in front of us."

18

Evan's mother felt the fluttering in his finger first and she quickly raised her head off the hospital bed to find Evan looking at her with tired eyes.

"Evan!" Connie Nash gasped, jumping to her feet and wrapping her arms around him. She squeezed him briefly before pushing back and looking down into his gray-blue eyes. Her chin trembled as she started to cry.

A weak grin spread across Evan's dry lips. "Hi, Mom." After a pause, he wrinkled his brow and looked around the room. "Where am I?"

His mother quickly wiped the tears from her eyes and cleared her throat. "You're at the hospital."

Evan stared at her, processing the answer. "The hospital?" he replied quietly. "What happened?"

She held back an impulse to roll her eyes. Where was she supposed to start? She decided to keep it simple. "You had another episode."

He blinked several times, trying to remember. He looked down at his hand and turned it over to reveal the tape and the IV line on the other side. "How long have I been here?"

"About a day and a half," she said.

"What day is it?"

"Tuesday." Connie brushed some hair away from his eyes.

Evan glimpsed a look of nervousness on his mother's face. He closed his eyes, trying to think, and then promptly opened them again. "How did I get here?"

Connie frowned. She knew this was coming but still struggled with the answer. The simplest answer, she thought, was usually the first one.

She moved her hand down and placed it on his. "Your episode was in Dr. Mayer's office. She called an ambulance."

Over Evan's head, the heart rate monitor suddenly showed an increase in tempo. All at once, it came rushing back to him. He'd had another episode, and it was on her couch. That's why she called an ambulance. Something must have gone wrong, which meant he hadn't *controlled* it after all.

Evan's eyes widened. "Where's Dr. Mayer?"

His mother squeezed his hand. "Easy," she said. "Don't worry about any of this right now. You just need to get better."

He shook his head. "Mom, she needs to know I'm okay."

"Honey, she'll find out," she replied soothingly. "Right now you need to be resting, not worrying about that woman."

"That woman?" Evan asked, with a puzzled expression. "What does that mean?"

"Nothing, I just meant . . . she'll find out."

Evan blinked again, watching his mother. Something was wrong. "Mom, tell me what happened."

"Nothing," she said, trying to quiet him.

"Something happened. I can see it. What happened? *What happened to Dr. Mayer?"*

This time his mother did roll her eyes. She and her son knew each other too well. "If you have to know, I asked her to leave," she explained with a firm voice.

Evan raised his eyebrows. "She was here and you made her leave? Why?"

His mother sat on the edge of his bed and stared at him. Finally, she took a deep breath. "Evan, your episodes have been getting worse. You know that, right?"

He didn't answer.

"Well, she did too. And she continued helping facilitate them while knowing they were getting worse. She kept doing it, knowing *you* were getting worse."

"Mom, she was trying to help me," Evan replied, shaking his head.

"No, Evan," her voice grew louder, "she was trying to help herself and at your expense." She continued in response to Evan's confused expression. "She admitted it all to her sister. She didn't know I was standing behind her when she admitted she was helping you with the hope that whatever you were seeing could somehow tell her something about her daughter. She was using you, Evan. She was using you the whole time!"

Evan remained silent, watching the anger grow in his mother. He let the weight of his head fall back into his thick pillow. "I know that."

Connie looked at her son incredulously. "What!"

"I said I know. I know she was using me."

"You knew?" She stared at her son, confused. "How?"

"Because it was my idea."

"What?"

"It was my idea, mom."

His mother was stunned. She looked at her son, trying to comprehend what he had just said. "I don't . . . why?"

Evan's eyes softened, and he shrugged. "You've always told me we're supposed to help people."

His mother's eyes widened with surprise. "My God, Evan, not when it risks your own life!" She leaned forward and squeezed his hand. "Why on earth would you do something so dangerous?"

He lowered his gaze to the bed and his covered legs. He wasn't about to bring up his sister. "Do you remember when I was little, and Uncle Rick took us to Disneyland?"

"Yes."

"Remember when I got lost?"

She remembered it vividly. He was five and had gotten mixed up after going into the men's restroom. He ended up coming out through the door on the opposite side, where she couldn't see him. "Yes," she nodded.

This time Evan gave her a weak squeeze of his own. "Do you remember how scared you were when you couldn't find me?"

How could she ever forget? "I do."

"How would you have felt if you'd *never* found me that day? If you never knew what happened." He watched his mother slowly close her eyes and lower her head. "I think that's how Dr. Mayer feels," he whispered.

His mother opened her eyes with tears in them. She placed her second hand on top of her son's and squeezed it harder.

"She cries every day, Mom. Every day."

Connie Nash looked back up to her son, pressing her lips firmly together, fighting back the tears. "We all cry, Evan."

He gave his mother a pained look. "Not like this."

19

The doctor glared at the two women with disdain, but finally lowered the shotgun. "What do you want?"

The women looked at each other. They took a few steps forward. "We need to talk to you."

Reluctantly, Rief raised the shotgun up and laid it over his shoulder. "Not here. Inside." He climbed the steps to the porch and opened the door. Looking back, he saw the two women take a deep breath and follow him up the wide steps.

In all the excitement, Mary had forgotten how crisp it was outside until they walked into the small log cabin. In the corner was a woodstove, glowing orange inside. Next to it was a small, clean kitchen with a wooden table near the window. On their left was a larger sitting area with a hallway leading to the rear. The A-frame ceiling rose high above their heads.

Rief motioned the women to a couch against the wall and took a seat in front of them. He kept the gun laying across his lap. The angry look on his face was replaced by one of distrust.

"How did you find me?" he asked.

"From a doctor at the hospital, Dr. Bailey. He said you used to go fishing together a long time ago." She barely finished the sentence when Rief spoke again.

"What are your names?"

Mary leaned forward. "My name is Mary Creece and this is Sue Bales. Like I said, we're from Los Angeles."

Rief stared at Sue for a long time before turning back. "What are you doing here?"

"We're looking for you," Mary answered. "You *are* Dr. Rief?"

He gave her a subtle, reluctant nod.

"We're hoping you can help us."

He didn't say anything, so Sue retrieved something from her jacket pocket, unfolded it, and laid it down on the rectangular coffee table between them. She softly slapped it in place to add effect. "Recognize this?" she asked. It was the page from the medical journal containing the case Rief had documented.

"Where did you get that?"

"From a friend," Sue replied. "A collector. Very few of those journals are around anymore."

He didn't respond.

Mary leaned forward. "We want to talk to you about Dan Taylor. The patient you submitted this case about."

A look of grief passed through the doctor's eyes. "Daniel Taylor is dead."

"We know that," said Sue. "But we're hoping you know something that we don't."

"We have a young man in the hospital," added Mary, "a kid, who has symptoms very similar to what you described in 1982. He's in ICU right now, and we're afraid he's not going to make it out. We're praying you can help us."

They watched Rief reach forward and pick up the sheet of paper. He held it up with a look of painful recognition. After a few minutes, he silently put it back down on the table. "Daniel was just a kid too."

"We know you tried to save him," Mary offered.

He almost smirked. "Do you?" He shook his head with a sigh and leaned back in his chair. "I *couldn't* save him. I tried. But it happened too fast. His body . . . just . . . kept getting weaker. There was nothing I could do."

Mary looked at him curiously. "How fast?"

He shrugged. "Less than a month."

"Oh, my God," she whispered under her breath.

"He was in a car accident," Rief continued. "He wasn't wearing a seatbelt and his head hit the windshield. Initially, it looked like a concussion but he seemed to recover well enough."

Mary leaned forward. "The symptoms you documented; when did they begin?"

"Not immediately. In the beginning, Daniel said he was okay and I believed him. But then he told me he had started seeing things. It was only days later."

"What things did he see?"

Rief didn't answer. He gazed past them as the pain flooded back. "I didn't believe him. I thought he was just a little delusional, that it was remnants of the shock from the accident. It takes time for shock to wear off." He looked back at them. "I told Daniel he just needed to give it time. Give it time, I told him. That was exactly what he didn't have.

"I kept thinking he'd be okay until he showed up in the emergency room one night. His roommate said he found him unconscious and barely breathing." Rief glanced absently to the floor. "I sat with him that whole night, cursing myself for not listening more closely to what he'd said."

Mary lowered her voice. "Did he wake up?"

"Yes," Rief answered, his head still down. "Yes, he did. And that time I listened! The frequency of the visions had increased, and he couldn't stop them. I was able to help but only a little. It quickly became evident that all I could really do was temporarily slow the problem."

Mary's eyes flashed a look of hope. "You slowed it down? How?"

Rief sighed. "Valium. Whatever was happening in Daniel's head was taking a deadly toll on his body. By keeping him slightly sedated, the trauma to his body was less severe. It looked like it was working. Until it stopped." Rief returned his gaze to Mary. "When the Valium was no longer effective, the physical trauma got even worse. As if somehow the drug accelerated the trauma. I didn't know what to do. I called everyone I knew, but their ideas were no better. That's when I submitted my review article to that journal out of desperation. By then I was praying for a miracle, hoping someone had seen it before."

"Did anyone answer you?"

"It didn't matter," Rief replied dryly. "Daniel Taylor fell into a coma and died a week later, before the article was ever published."

"I don't understand," Mary said, puzzled. "How could Valium make it *worse*; it's a sedative more than anything else."

He frowned. "Well, I don't think it actually made it worse. I think instead it masked the problem. More specifically, it gave the impression his physical symptoms were normalizing, when in reality they were getting worse. Much worse."

The room fell silent, and Mary shook her head in disbelief. "Are you telling us there's nothing we can do to stop this? That Evan's just going to die?"

Rief glanced from Mary to Sue, then sighed. "Look, I don't know what your kid has, but if it's the same thing, then yes, that's exactly what I'm suggesting."

Mary was incredulous. "There has to be something we can do."

"If there is, I don't know what it is," Rief said, shaking his head. "Maybe you can stall it longer than I did. I've lived all these years with the realization that I only sped up Daniel's death. Perhaps if I'd given him something more specific, like Prozac or another anti-psychotic, it would have helped. It's a question I've asked myself a million times."

Sue looked at Mary, who was staring back at her with a raised eyebrow.

Rief watched them and thought for a moment. "Has this boy Evan taken any drugs yet?"

"Not that I know of."

"Good, don't let him. Keep him clean. It might buy you enough time to learn something new. Whatever you do, *don't* put any drugs in him."

20

Shannon Mayer sat hunched forward, her face down on her desk. Her hands, crossed, lay over her head, while tears rolled off her cheeks and onto the polished wood. She couldn't hold it together anymore. She had reached the end of her rope.

Shannon had come into the office in a desperate attempt to maintain the veneer of confidence she had worn at work over the last eighteen months. Wearing that mask had allowed her, at the least, to *function*, but with each passing day, it hid less and less. And now, she couldn't even manage that. It was over. She was breaking down.

She couldn't hear the footsteps in the hall over the sound of her sobbing and was startled when the doorknob on her office door began to turn. She heard the loud click and barely had time to lift her head from the desk before the door opened. Shannon sat up and wiped her face as the last person she ever expected walked into the room. It was Evan's mother, Connie Nash.

Shannon peered at the woman through blurry eyes, and almost leapt from her chair. She quickly came around her desk but was stopped when the woman silently held up her hand.

She watched Connie step to the side and was utterly stunned when Evan came through the door next, leaning heavily on Tania's shoulder. When they got far enough inside, Connie let the door go and it quietly closed behind them.

Shannon stared at Evan standing weakly before her, visibly struggling to remain erect. It took her a few tries before she could form the words to speak to him.

"Evan," she whispered. "What on earth?"

Tania kept an arm around Evan's waist as his mother stepped back in to support him from the other side. With an arm around each of his escorts, Evan smiled meekly at Dr. Mayer.

"He wouldn't let me tell you he was coming," Tania said, in apology.

Shannon looked at Tania then turned back to Evan, trying to understand. She began to cry again. "My God, you're all right!"

Connie Nash forced herself to refrain from making the snide remark that she was thinking.

Even in his weakened condition, Evan looked at Shannon with concern. "Are you okay?"

"Are *you*?" She almost scolded. Her chastising tone was quickly followed by a sense of guilt. "I'm so sorry, Evan. I am *so sorry!*"

"It's not your fault," he said quietly, as his mother and Tania helped him down onto the large couch. His breathing was shallow and labored. "I thought I could handle it," he said. "But it happened too fast."

"It doesn't matter." Shannon stepped forward in front of him. "The important thing is you're alive."

Evan nodded slowly. "I know. But I think I know what to do next time."

Next time? Shannon stared at him, startled. *What did he just say?* She turned to his mother, who was glaring bitterly at her.

"What?"

Evan pushed his hands against the couch and adjusted his position with a grimace. "I think I know how to keep it under control."

"What in the world are you talking about!"

Evan took a deep breath and looked up at her. "We have to do it again."

She couldn't believe her ears. She glanced back at his mother, who continued to grit her teeth in silence. "E-Evan," Shannon stammered. "Are you crazy? There is no way in hell we're going to do that again. You almost didn't—"

"We have to!" he said louder, interrupting her. He looked into her eyes, trying to hide some of his exhaustion.

"My God, why?"

"Because I think your daughter Ellie is *alive*."

21

Sam Roa stood confidently in his new sweater vest and slacks, scanning the kitchen and dining room. Everything had been carefully wiped clean and boxed up. The counters and shelves were as clean as he had ever seen them. No traces.

The living room was the same. The old couch and upholstered chair had been vacuumed and wrapped in plastic. Everything else had been boxed and stacked along the wall or thrown out long ago. Every surface in the house had been wiped down thoroughly with Lysol. No germs, no dust, and especially no fingerprints.

It was almost time and he was ready. He had chosen the smallest church in town and given them the story he'd practiced. He was leaving the area, moving south to take care of his dying sister, and wanted to donate his property to a church that could use it. And with things being such a hardship, he chose to leave most of his things behind for the church to sell for the proceeds. It was his way of giving back to the community that he cherished so much.

Of course, it was also a way to confuse the authorities with regard to any evidence he might have missed. A fingerprint, an address, a bill, anything that might indicate where he may have gone would hopefully be distributed well enough to prevent any investigation—even as unlikely as that was to occur—from turning up any useful information too soon.

Even better was the agreement that the church would bulldoze his old house and begin construction of a larger, modernized hall for its congregation. With the large plot of land, the church would have more than enough space to create the house of worship it had always longed for. They were deeply grateful for the donation, which Roa privately dismissed. What was far more valuable to him was the church's agreement to bulldoze the site immediately after he left. In fact, it was especially important since Roa's house had one unique attribute. With Southern California's notoriously warm weather, very few houses had what his did: one of the only full basements in the entire county.

Roa took one more satisfied look and then strode down the hall to a large metal door. He quietly opened it and peered down the dimly lit stairs. Closing the door behind him, he descended to the bottom and noted how eerie the empty basement now looked. The old gas heater stood solemnly in the corner, set off by the gray concrete floor and walls all around. He reflected on how much time he'd spent down there. After all, nothing dampened sound quite as well as good old-fashioned concrete.

Roa turned and approached the only door in the room that led to the second half of the basement, which was entirely closed off from the rest. Next to the door a flat monitor was mounted on the wall. He turned the monitor on. He would soon have to disassemble and remove it, as it was one of the few key things he absolutely could not allow the church, or anyone else, to discover.

The monitor lit up and displayed the room on the other side of the thick wall. It had no windows and just the single large door, outside of which Roa now stood. The room also had a low-light camera, which was wired to his monitor.

Inside the room, Ellie Mayer sat quietly in the corner. She played with her small doll, bouncing it lightly on her lap and quietly whispering to it as she played with its blonde hair. It wasn't something an eight-year-old would normally play with, but she had few choices.

The young girl was dressed in new clothes, and her brown hair was tied back into a ponytail with a pink elastic band.

Behind Ellie, against the clean white wall, was a twin-sized bed frame and mattress. A small white and pink dresser stood beside the bed. Not far from the bed was a small toilet and sink. A thick multi-colored rug dressed the cold, tiled floor and several more toys and books were gathered in the corner. It was all that was left after the man had removed almost everything else.

Roa watched her for a long time, as he always did, until she eventually set the doll aside and picked up one of the other toys, a brown stuffed dog. It was nice finally seeing her enjoy herself. For a long time, she had fought back, constantly screaming and throwing fits. He'd visited her several times every day without fail, but she had wanted nothing to do with him. The first year was hard for both of them but things did eventually subside. Of course, it was only recently that she had actually begun talking to him.

In fact, she'd talked to him more in the last two months than in the entire first year with him. She had even begun calling him by his first name. It filled Roa with a deep optimism for what he was about to do.

———•———

Ellie continued playing nonchalantly with her dog, waiting. Finally, she heard the familiar creaking of the wooden stairs, which told her he was headed back up. He didn't know, but there *were* some things she could hear through the walls. After detecting the faint sound of the door closing at the top, she put the stuffed animal down and picked up a pail of blocks. She carefully slid her hand down the inside and pulled up what was hidden at the bottom.

—•—

Upstairs, Roa traveled down the hallway toward the back of the house. He paused, then decisively pushed a door open and stepped inside a small room. The largest wall was completely covered with photographs, from different angles and places, but all of the same person. They were the last things to remove and burn.

He stared at the wall absently, going through the details in his head. Had he missed anything? He'd signed the donation papers for the house. The car was being donated to another charity, and the electricity would be shut off in twenty-four hours. The passports, reservations, clothes, and traveler's checks were all ready.

Eighteen months had been an agonizingly long wait, but he couldn't risk being spotted until Ellie's face had long faded from the public's memory. And now, not only would she cooperate, but with her recent turnaround regarding him, his original plan was beginning to shift altogether.

They were hours away.

22

Shannon Mayer's face turned ashen. Her legs suddenly wobbled and gave out, and she fell to the floor. Tania gasped and jumped to her side. She bent down and wrapped an arm around Shannon, just in time to prevent the rest of her body from falling to the carpet.

"Dr. Mayer! Are you all right? Did you faint?"

Shannon, still on her knees, swayed back and forth. She was staring deliriously at Evan.

Tania, still clutching Shannon, realized what Evan had just said. "Ellie's alive?"

Evan turned to Tania. "I think so." He looked worriedly at Shannon, who was staring at him in shock. "I saw her but only for a second. I have to go back."

Evan's mother watched Shannon struggle to steady herself, even with Tania's help, and finally Connie knelt down to help them. She was reluctantly losing her anger toward Shannon, beginning to see the woman not as some kind of monster, but as a mother who had been put through an emotional torture that few could understand.

Evan watched Shannon, still on her knees, eyes fixed, and blinking repeatedly. "Dr. Mayer, are you okay?"

Did she hear correctly what he had said?

Yes, Shannon had heard. His words were still ringing in her ears. The very words for which she had prayed every single day. *Ellie is alive.*

"She's alive?" Shannon asked weakly. Her lips were trembling. "Are you sure?"

Evan opened his mouth but stopped before he let the words out, struck by a terrifying thought. *What if he was wrong?* What if he was wrong and just mistakenly told Dr. Mayer that her daughter was alive? *But . . . he saw her. He saw her just for a moment, but it was her. Wasn't it?* He was afraid to exhale, suddenly afraid of answering her. How could he be sure? All he had seen were some pictures. He quickly backpedaled through his thoughts, through the memory of what he had seen. *No! No!* He felt a surge of emotion and Ellie's image came rushing back into his mind.

"It was her," he said confidently. "I saw her. She's alive." And then he hesitated. "But I have to go back. Something is happening."

Shannon's face quickly grew concerned. "W-what does that mean?"

"I don't know." Evan shook his head nervously. "But I saw . . . boxes, boxes in an empty house. And I saw *suitcases.*"

Everyone's eyes grew wide. Shannon turned and frantically reached for the phone on her desk. She had her hand on the receiver when she stopped herself. Her first instinct was to call her husband, Dennis, to tell him, to save him from the emotional hell he had fallen into before it was too late.

But she couldn't, at least not yet. She stared at the receiver still in her hand. *What if Evan was wrong? What if Ellie wasn't . . .*

She turned back to Evan. "Can you find her?"

He thought for a moment, then shook his head hesitantly. "I don't know. I can try."

His mother spoke up nervously. "Evan, this could kill you."

Evan shook his head. "It won't." He turned to Shannon. "Dr. Mayer, I know what it is that's causing my problems. When I see the fog, my body . . . panics. Not my mind, my body. It panics at the fear that it won't come back out. But I think we can stop it."

"What do you mean?"

"Well, maybe not stop it but slow it down. My body, I mean. Like a sedative or something. You can give out medicine, right?"

Shannon squinted at him. "But you hate drugs."

The corner of Evan's mouth curled slightly. "Not today, I don't."

Shannon raised an eyebrow at his mother. "Ms. Nash?"

Evan's mother glanced worriedly at her son, then back to Shannon. Finally, she dropped her head and nodded.

Shannon stood up carefully. There *was* something they could use. It was strong and safe and would definitely relax him. "Okay. But the second the symptoms start," she said, "we're waking you up!"

"Deal." Evan put one hand on the arm of the couch and pushed himself onto his feet. "There is one other thing," he said with a pause. "To do it quickly, I don't think those pictures are going to work. I need something with a stronger connection to Ellie."

23

Mary sat in the passenger seat gazing out the window as they turned off the dirt road and headed back toward the interstate. She felt empty inside. She leaned her head against the cold window and closed her eyes, thinking what a failure their trip was. They came to find a way to help Evan, but what they were leaving with was more likely a death sentence for the boy.

They could try to delay the inevitable, hoping to find a solution, but neither of them was feeling very optimistic. For all the effort it took to find him, Rief, in the end, gave them the worst possible news.

After going back over Rief's words in her mind, Mary was the first to speak after they left. She could still visualize the doctor watching from his doorway as they drove away.

"You know," Mary said, trying to find a glimmer of hope. "Maybe he's just wrong. Maybe Daniel Taylor had something different than what Evan does. Or maybe it was worse."

Sue kept her eyes on the road, listening. Her cell phone chirped and she looked down at the center console to see a new text message appear. A moment later it chirped again. She glanced at Mary, then checked her rearview mirror before slowing and pulling to the side of the road. She stopped the car on the gravel shoulder, and promptly pushed the gearshift forward into park.

Sue picked up her phone. "Got two more messages from the office."

Mary turned and looked out the window. "I mean what if Rief got it wrong? Just because the symptoms are the same doesn't mean the cause is the same. Besides, he hasn't practiced in what, twenty years?" She watched the trees outside sway in the cold wind. "He didn't even know the difference between an antidepressant and antipsychotic. Right?"

Sue finished reading the two messages and looked up over the steering wheel with a strange expression. She quickly turned to Mary. "Wait, what did you just say?"

"Didn't you catch that? Rief said he should have tried giving Taylor a 'Prozac or another antipsychotic,' like they were the same thing. They're not. Antidepressants are very different. What I'm saying is maybe he didn't even diagnose the kid correctly. Jeez, Sue."

Sue's eyes opened wider.

Mary continued: "What if he just wasn't a very good doctor? Maybe there's still hope for Evan, maybe—"

Mary suddenly stopped when she saw Sue's face. "What?"

"Prozac is just a trade name for fluoxetine, Mary. And fluoxetine was already coming on the scene in the '80s. But *antipsychotics* were developed long before that."

Mary tilted her head with curiosity. "And?"

Sue blinked, still thinking. "And . . . Dr. Rief should have known the difference."

"Well, like I said, maybe he wasn't very *good*."

"No," Sue said, shaking her head. "You don't have your own practice if you're not very good. At least not back then you didn't." She looked out the window, still thinking. "We have to go back!"

"What?"

Sue put the car in drive again and made a tight U-turn across the road. "We have to go back."

Mary held on as Sue stepped hard on the accelerator. "Why?"

"Because there's more to this story!"

"How do you know that?"

As she gripped the steering wheel, Sue replied, "Read the message I just got on my phone."

———•———

Shannon drove cautiously up her long driveway. She parked in front of her house, and couldn't decide whether she was relieved or concerned when she saw her husband's truck gone.

She and Tania jumped out of the car and opened the back doors to help Evan out. His mother followed, still holding onto him. Evan grabbed the top of the door and pulled himself up onto his feet. For a moment, his frailty, coupled with his small size, made him appear far older than he was.

He took a deep breath and straightened. Feeling his mother's arm under his, he walked forward toward the front door. Even in his weakened state, he noted how beautiful the house was.

Shannon opened the door and walked ahead down a marble-tiled hallway, calling out for her husband, Dennis. There was no answer. She quickly returned to the others and directed them up the wide spiral staircase, then down the upstairs hallway, where she gingerly pushed open the door to Ellie's room.

Evan stopped and scanned the room, looking at the walls and then over Ellie's small dresser and bookcase. "This is better." His eyes fell on her bed, which was covered with a light-green comforter. He turned to Shannon with a questioning look, and she nodded back.

He stepped forward, then turned and lowered himself onto the edge of the bed.

"Do you need anything, Evan?"

He looked back up at Shannon and shook his head. "We need to hurry," Evan said.

Shannon quickly opened her purse and withdrew a small plastic bottle. She popped the cap off and dumped a single large pill into her palm. "This is a Valium," she said, handing it to him. "It's pretty powerful, especially for your size, but very safe."

Evan examined the tan-colored tablet in his hand, while Tania ducked out to get some water. She returned a minute later and handed the glass to him. He gave her a weak smile and took the glass, quickly swallowing the pill and washing it down.

His mother placed the pillow under his head as Evan laid himself down onto the small bed. When he looked up, he couldn't help but chuckle at all three women standing over him, almost shoulder to shoulder.

He reached out and squeezed his mom's hand.

"Ms. Nash," Shannon said, stepping behind her and placing her hand on Evan's forehead. "I want you to keep your hand on his head. If you feel any change in temperature, tell me immediately."

"Okay."

Shannon knelt down next to Evan. She slipped off her watch, and placed her fingertips lightly on his wrist. "I'll monitor his pulse. Tania, I want you to watch his breathing. If his diaphragm starts moving faster, tell us."

Finally, Shannon looked at Evan. "At the first sign of *anything*, we're pulling you out."

"Hopefully you won't have to hit me again," Evan said with a smile. He was already beginning to feel tired, unsure whether it was the Valium or exhaustion. With the calming effect of his mother's hand on his head, he closed his eyes and thought of his regret about not telling them the whole truth. He couldn't. If they knew what image was *really* panicking his system, they never would have agreed; no matter how much danger Ellie was in.

—•—

It didn't take long before Evan felt the Valium kick in. He could feel the gradual withdrawal of his senses a few minutes before he slipped under. The darkness seeped in from all around as the exhaustion tried to overtake him, and he struggled to hold onto his thoughts. Then he saw it.

The cool white wisps began to appear out of the darkness. They grew from the edges and swirled inward, until touching and weaving into a thick shroud.

He was having trouble thinking now, as the medication pushed him further and further from awareness. He fought to hang on to the vision, waiting. Finally, the fog started to move and began to open. Ever so slowly, the middle thinned until a faint outline could be seen beyond it. He continued fighting, straining to see what the outline defined. It became progressively clearer and eventually began to resemble . . . tiles.

He pushed forward, searching for greater clarity, as the vision continued to grow. The square shapes became larger until they looked less like tiles and more like frames. Then something was moving. He couldn't see what it was at first, but it continued to sharpen into focus until he recognized it: a man.

Then he fumbled and his concentration began to slip, but not before he spotted it. The fear. The terror.

In an instant, the fog began to change shape and the red background began to bleed through. The picture . . .

—•—

"Evan! Evan, can you hear me! *EVAN!*"

He felt his head suddenly jerk from side to side, and realized someone was shaking him hard. He tried to open his eyes but couldn't. The screaming and shaking continued, harder.

"*EVAN!*"

He forced his eyes open and was awash in blinding light, as the screaming voice of his mother became clearer.

Evan searched for his mother through narrowed eyes until he found her face hovering over him. He gasped and convulsed, then rolled violently onto his side and off the bed, hitting the floor with a thud. He could feel hands surrounding him and helping to raise him onto his knees just before he heaved and threw up.

"Oh, God!" cried his mother's voice.

"Get him away!"

Evan's mother and Tania pulled him away, while Shannon grabbed the comforter from the bed and threw it over the mess on the floor.

He collapsed and rolled onto his back, coughing violently. His mother had just wiped his mouth with something when Evan held up his hand, telling her to give him a minute. His eyesight was coming back and, after a few minutes, the heaving in his chest subsided. A tear rolled down his left cheek, and he gave one last fitful cough before gently lowering his head back down onto the carpet.

"Evan, are you all right?"

"I'm okay."

Shannon's face appeared above him. "Are you sure?"

He nodded. "Yes."

She looked at the others, then back down at him, anxiously. "Did you see anything?"

He nodded again. "It was a room, with someone in it. And there was a wall, covered with *pictures*."

"Was it Ellie in the room?" Shannon asked, excitedly.

"No, it was a man. He was taking them down."

"They were pictures? Pictures of what?"

Evan swallowed hard. "They were all pictures of the same person. *Pictures of you.*"

24

"What?!"

"The pictures were of you, Dr. Mayer," Evan repeated.

Shannon was confused. "Pictures of me? What does that mean?"

"I don't know."

"How many were there?"

Evan took a deep breath. "Hundreds."

"I don't understan—" Shannon suddenly stopped. She turned her head, thinking. "Wait a minute," she turned back to Evan. "You said there was a man in the room. What did he look like?"

Evan shook his head. "I'm not sure. I could only see him from the back. He was bald and big. Muscular."

Everyone watched the blood drain from Shannon's face. She sat motionless on her knees, gazing at him.

"No," she whispered. *"No!"*

Evan's mother looked down at her son, then back to Shannon. "What is it?"

"It can't be," Shannon mumbled. *It's impossible!* But in an instant, all the pieces fell into place. She leapt up and ran out of the room, down the carpeted hallway. When she reached the next doorway, she ran across her master bedroom to a small filing cabinet in the corner and yanked it open. With a look of dread, she thumbed through the folders as quickly as she could. She finally stopped and pulled a file out, flipping it open.

Shannon ran back down the hall to Evan and turned the folder around to show him. On the first page were several paragraphs of personal information, but it was the photograph in the upper left-hand corner that caught Evan's attention. The picture was of a large, muscular man, staring intently into the camera. He looked to be in his forties and was bald.

"Is this the man?"

Evan studied the photograph. "I'm not sure. I saw him from the back. But his shape looks the same." He looked up at her quizzically. "You know him?"

Shannon straightened and stood up. Her previous look of hopelessness and despair was now changing into something else entirely. "Yes, I know him!"

My God it was him. But how? The police had cleared him. They said he had an alibi. All this time . . . all this time they thought it was someone trying to get back at her husband, because he was a police officer. They could not have been more wrong. And now, now she knew why she'd felt like she was running out of time.

She looked back down at Evan. "And you said you saw suitcases?"

He nodded. "I think he's getting ready to leave. As in soon."

Shannon grabbed her purse and pulled out her phone. She quickly dialed her husband's number and held it to her ear. After multiple rings, it rolled to voice mail. "Dennis, where are you? Call me! It's about Ellie!" She hung up and quickly redialed. It went to voice mail again.

She hung up and dialed her sister's number. There was no answer. "Dammit!" Shannon looked around the room frantically. "I'm going!" She grabbed her purse and headed for the door.

"Wait!" Evan shouted. When Shannon turned around, he could see anger in her eyes. He glanced over his shoulder at his mother, who nodded. "We're coming too!"

"Oh, no you're not!"

Evan struggled to his feet, again with the help of Tania and his mother. "Yes, we are. You need help."

Shannon stared at him for a long moment, deliberating. She surprised Evan when she crossed the room and took Tania's place under his arm. She hated to admit it, but if they really were running out of time, they had to find the right house, fast. The address she had in the man's folder was old, and if they were somewhere else, Evan might be able to help her figure out where.

"Tania," she ordered, "you stay here. Get on the phone and *find my husband!*"

They rushed out of the room, carrying Evan, while Tania ran into the master bedroom and grabbed the home phone.

In Ellie's room, the green comforter remained strewn across the floor, covering the mess that Evan had made. Had someone taken a second look, they would have realized just how much of the mess was actually blood.

—•—

Dennis Mayer was less than ten miles away, sitting in his truck at the top of a large hill. He was looking out across the city of Los Angeles and watching the sun slip slowly down below the horizon. As darkness fell, he sat in silence, trying to think of a reason for being alive.

He had failed his wife and his daughter, the two people who meant the most to him. The only people who mattered. He turned and looked outside at the trees with their fluttering leaves, then the clouds, and finally the last of the sunset. Everything around him, the entire world, seemed gray and distant.

His baby girl was gone. Taken by someone who hated him and wanted to show him how real pain felt. Well, it had worked. His family was destroyed, and so was his very will to live. Whoever it was, he'd won and knew it. Mayer didn't know what he had done to deserve this. But whatever it was, he now accepted it.

The sound of his cell phone rang out and he turned to look at it on the seat beside him. It was a call from Shannon. He stared at it, then reached over and turned the phone off. She would understand.

Dennis Mayer placed the phone back on the seat and picked up the handgun that lay next to it. The familiar steel in his hand felt so natural. With a smooth motion, he pulled the slide back; a bullet entered the chamber.

Shannon would understand.

25

Sue brought the car to a skidding stop in front of the cabin and both women jumped out, running toward the steps.

"Are you sure about this?" Mary yelled.

"Trust me!"

Sue reached the top of the stairs first and pounded on the front door. Seconds later, the door swung open and Rief stepped out.

"Now what?"

Sue said nothing. Instead, she pushed her way past him into the house, pulling Mary along with her.

"What the hell are you doing?" Rief growled, and slammed the door behind them. Both he and Mary turned to watch Sue, who was intently scanning the room. She finally spun back around to face him. "Well?"

He looked back and forth between them. "Well, what?"

Sue folded her arms in front of her. "Would you like to start, or shall I?"

Rief, puzzled, scanned the room trying to figure out what she was referring to. He shook his head. "I have no idea what you're talking about."

Sue turned her glare away and looked at Mary. "Go ahead, Mary."

Mary was studying Rief's face but couldn't tell whether he was acting. She put her hands on her hips. "Prozac."

"What?"

"Prozac," she repeated.

Rief shook his head again. "Prozac what?"

"You said Prozac was an antipsychotic. It's not. It's an antidepressant."

He squinted at her, still confused. "So what? I made a mistake."

"Maybe, but that's like a doctor saying aspirin is an anti-inflammatory."

"Who the hell cares! Christ, it was over twenty years ago."

"Exactly," said Sue.

Rief now focused on her.

"It was over twenty years ago," she continued. "About the time you last saw your fishing buddy. What was his name again?"

Rief continued squinting, trying to understand where she was going.

"His name was Baily, remember?"

"I remember," Rief answered.

Sue smirked. "I'm not sure that you did. When Mary told you about him, you didn't show the slightest reaction to his name."

Rief folded his own arms across his chest, but said nothing.

Sue turned and looked around the room again. "For a man who likes to fish, I don't see a single fishing item. No souvenirs, no fish mounted on the wall, no pictures. Nothing."

"You came back here because I don't have a fish on the wall?"

"No, we came back here because you don't have any pictures of your fishing trips. Not you, not your friends, no one. In fact, you don't have any pictures of anyone *at all*."

Rief shrugged, irritated. "I'm not sentimental."

"That, I believe. But we're not talking about sentimentality, are we?" she smiled sarcastically and paused. "Weren't you *married*?"

Mary watched as Rief began to grow noticeably uncomfortable.

"Yes, I was married. My wife died a long time ago."

"Before you met Daniel Taylor?"

"Yes, as a matter of fact."

Sue kept her gaze on Rief. "Mary, have you ever met a widower who didn't keep pictures of his wife?"

Mary shook her head. "Not without being remarried."

"And are you remarried, Mr. Rief?"

Rief didn't even make an effort to answer.

"So I'm getting that either you're heartless or you didn't want anyone to see those pictures. And I'm leaning toward the latter."

Rief was beginning to look angry. "What the hell do you want from me?"

"How about the truth?"

He glared at both of them. "You have no idea what you're talking about."

"Don't I?" Sue leveled her gaze at him. "How old are you?"

"How old am I? Why do—"

"HOW OLD ARE YOU?" she yelled.

Rief jumped, surprised, but didn't answer.

"Mary, how old would you guess Mr. Rief to be?"

"Mmm . . . I would say mid-fifties."

Sue nodded. "Exactly what I was thinking. But Dr. Rief had his own practice in the '80s, and to have his own practice back then meant he was probably at least in his forties. Which means today he should be about seventy years old. I'd say he looks awfully good for seventy, wouldn't you?"

Mary grinned. "Smashing."

Sue stepped closer to Rief. "It was Mary that caught it; your Prozac mistake. After that, a lot of inconsistencies in your story began to appear."

"Oh my God!" Mary gasped, suddenly piecing it all together. "You're not Dr. Rief at all. You're *Daniel Taylor*!"

—•—

Both women were back on the couch, staring intently at him.

"Is *anything* you told us the truth?"

Taylor sat slouched in his chair with a hand propped up, covering part of his mouth. After a long silence, he calmly dropped his hand and retrieved a pack of cigarettes from his shirt pocket. "Yes." He slid one out and put it between his lips, then pulled out a lighter.

"Which part?" Mary asked.

He looked at her with a slight roll of his eyes. "That your kid Evan is living on borrowed time." He lit up and dropped the lighter back into his pocket.

Both women looked at each other. "Well, if *you're* alive, then it can't be terminal."

"Don't bet on it. It sounds like it's progressing faster in him. I had weeks; he has days, maybe hours." Taylor watched as what little optimism the women had left evaporated. "I'm sorry to tell you that. But if it's any consolation, his life would be far worse if he lived."

"How on earth can you say that?"

"Because they'll find him," Taylor replied dryly.

The women were confused. "Who's going to find him?"

"*Them.*"

"Who's 'them'?"

"The same ones who found me." He took another drag from his cigarette.

Neither woman was following. "Who are you talking about? Who found you?"

He sighed. "Rief was a good man. He was trying to help me. But neither of us knew at the time that it was the worst thing he could have done." Taylor leaned his head back against the top of his chair. "He didn't know what to do. My symptoms weren't fatal yet, but they were getting progressively worse, and nothing he tried was working. When he submitted his article to that journal, he was hoping that someone, somewhere, had seen my problem before. But they hadn't."

"So, no one answered?" asked Mary.

"Oh, someone answered all right. And it was the worst possible answer." The women watched the tiny embers in the cigarette glow as he took another drag. "Someone read Rief's article, and they came in force."

"Who?"

"The CIA."

"What did the CIA want with you?" Mary asked.

Taylor almost laughed. "You are naïve, aren't you? I guess you really are nurses." He stopped, as if trying to decide something. Finally, he asked, "How much do you know about the government?"

Sue raised an eyebrow. "That's . . . kind of a broad question, isn't it?"

This time, Taylor let out a chuckle. "I guess it is. Have you ever heard about the Stargate Project?"

Both shook their heads.

"I didn't think so. Stargate was a secret project that began in the 1970s, primarily by the CIA." He shrugged. "You can read about it these days on the Internet. It was run by a bastard named Hollister. What they wanted to find out was whether psychic phenomenon was real, and whether it had any military applications. One such skill they tried to harness was called remote viewing. Ever hear of that?"

"No."

"Remote viewing is the practice, or should I say claim, of viewing unseen targets over some amount of distance. At least that's the official description. The CIA spent years trying to determine if it was legit. Most of the subjects were people they paid to come in to test. But a few people they brought in by force. People like me."

Taylor finished his cigarette and snuffed it out in an ashtray. "It didn't take long for the CIA to figure out that most of those people were frauds, looking to make some kind of name for themselves or just to make a few bucks. So imagine their surprise when they discovered some kid from Montana who could do it by accident. Better yet, who couldn't *stop* doing it."

"They kidnapped you?" Sue asked.

"Probably as good a word as any. It certainly wasn't elective."

"What happened?"

"Well, they damn near pissed their pants the first time I did it. I told them about something one of their fellow agents was doing in the other room. Then, after a few more episodes, they got really damn excited."

He fished another cigarette out. "The problem was that my symptoms were getting worse. I was getting sicker and sicker. But those 'spooks' didn't seem to care. They were so excited that they kept having me do it again and again. And I just got worse and worse."

"How long did they keep you?"

"A few weeks. When they saw me coughing up blood, they finally acknowledged there was a problem. I was dying, and quickly. And yet that was when the spooks *really* showed their true colors. You see, once they realized that I couldn't do it without dying on them, they did something that I never would have believed."

The women looked at Taylor expectantly.

"They decided the best thing to do was to operate and study me while they still could."

"Operate?" Mary asked. "Operate on what?"

"My brain. But, of course, they didn't mean *operate*. What they really meant was *dissect*."

Mary gasped. "What did you do?"

Taylor drew on his cigarette and exhaled slowly. "I found a way to escape and got the hell out of there."

Sue looked down at the table, listening intently. "So what happened to Dr. Rief?"

"I made it back to Butte and he hid me. We both realized that if I was going to live, it would be on the run, forever. But what Rief hadn't told me was that he had been diagnosed with cancer. I had no idea. Here he was trying to save me, while he was in the process of dying himself." Taylor shrugged. "I guess he felt guilty. But he shouldn't have."

"Maybe he just wanted to help one more person before dying," offered Mary.

Taylor looked at her through the rising stream of cigarette smoke, and gave a subtle nod. "Maybe."

Sue raised her head. "So you switched places!"

"We switched places," he acknowledged. "It took some effort, but we switched identities just before he died. And when Daniel Taylor was buried, it was in a closed casket."

"So you became Dr. Rief and left to hide away in the mountains?"

"Correct."

"Wow." Mary shook her head. "I mean, wow."

Sue slid forward on the couch. "Wait, if you're still hiding, that means you think someone is still looking for you."

"Correct again. My photograph and physical description are still in the system. With today's technology, it probably wouldn't take much for me to be spotted."

"So, did you steal Dr. Rief's information from Evelyn Sutton's house, his old landlord?"

"Yes. A long time ago."

"Tying up loose ends, I suppose?"

Taylor nodded. "More like destroying another path to find me."

Sue thought of something else and glared suspiciously at him. "You know, it wasn't long after 'you' supposedly died that the company who published that medical journal had their factory burn down. Was that a coincidence? After all, even with some journals already out there, it sure would be an effective way of keeping Dr. Rief's article contained."

He glanced at his cigarette and put it out half finished. "I'm sure I haven't the slightest idea what you're talking about." He glared back at the women. "So, now you know the truth. Now what?"

Mary sighed. "We still have to find a way to save Evan."

Taylor frowned. "It may be too late."

26

Shannon swerved frantically in and out of heavy traffic. Commuting hours on the Golden State Freeway were particularly bad, with miles of glowing red taillights.

Where the hell is the highway patrol when you need them? She held her phone up in front of her face to better see the redial button, and pressed it.

Tania answered after one ring.

"Anything?" Shannon pleaded, changing lanes.

"Not yet. I've left messages for your husband and your sister but haven't heard anything back."

"Dammit!" This was killing her. "Okay, call the Santa Clarita Sheriff's Department! Tell them we think a man named Samuel Roa kidnapped Ellie!" She flipped open the folder on the seat next to her and held up the paper with his photo on it. "His address is 301 Canyon Ridge Road. We need help right away!"

"Okay, I'm calling right now." Tania hung up.

Suddenly Shannon braked hard and swerved again, this time to avoid hitting a car in front of her.

"Who is Samuel Roa?"

Shannon glanced in the rearview mirror. Evan, who was leaning against his mother in the back seat, had put the question to her. "He was a patient of mine who had some posttraumatic problems after being discharged from the military." She changed back to the other lane. "But I had to stop seeing him. He started having issues with me as his doctor."

———•———

Captain Burnam turned off his computer, stood up, and grabbed his jacket. He glanced at his watch as he snaked one arm through the sleeve. He was going to be late. The door opened, and he turned around to see one of his female deputies lean in.

"Hey Cap'n, got a sec?"

"Sure, what's up?" He answered her while pulling the sides of his jacket together and zipping it up.

"We just got a call a few minutes ago from a young woman who says she has a lead on a kidnap case out of Glendale."

"Okay," said Burnam. "Is there a reason she's calling us?"

The deputy nodded. "Yeah. She says the woman she works for evidently thinks the person who kidnapped her kid lives here, out on Canyon Ridge."

"The woman she works for?"

"Right. The woman is a doctor, and this gal is apparently her receptionist."

Burnam looked at his deputy curiously. "If the doctor is the one with a missing kid, why is her receptionist calling?"

"She says the doctor is already in her car and on her way up here."

"Huh." Captain Burnam ran his tongue against the inside of his cheek. "Do we know who these people are?"

The deputy stepped inside and held up a piece of paper. "The doctor is Shannon Mayer, a psychiatrist from Glendale. The address she's headed to belongs to a man named Sam Roa."

Burnam looked at his watch again. "So the mother is driving to this guy Roa's house, thinking he has her kid?"

"That's what it sounds like."

"Why don't you run Roa's name through the system and see if anything turns up."

"I already did," the deputy answered, looking back down at her paper. "Roa moved here a little over four years ago after being dishonorably discharged from the Marines."

Burnam raised an eyebrow. "Is that right?"

"Yeah, but there's something else. He's got a restraining order out against him. And it's from that woman doctor."

"Christ." Burnam shook his head. "Okay, have someone run out there. Donaldson should be close. Hopefully he can get there before the woman does. In the meantime, find someone to send as backup."

"Right, okay."

The deputy turned and began to leave when Burnam stopped her. "And Becky, keep me up to date on my cell phone."

27

Sam Roa knelt down in front of the fireplace; feeding it a few pictures at a time and watching them quickly curl as they caught fire. Getting rid of the snapshots was harder for him than he had expected, but there could be no evidence.

Shannon Mayer was his whole life. She was the reason for all of it. Being discharged from the Marine Corps was bad enough, but losing his wife had shattered him. All he ever wanted to do was serve his country, to protect everything he held dear, but they sent him home instead. They sent him home in disgrace, claiming he had "psychological issues related to combat." Whatever the hell that meant.

Thank God for Shannon. Just when he was at the end of his rope, she volunteered to work with him, and for free. To help him out of his funk. But Roa could never have imagined what an angel the woman would turn out to be. For the first time, someone listened. For hours and hours, she listened to the horrors he'd had to endure, and she never judged. But most of all, she *cared*.

Having someone like Shannon showed Roa what life could be like, what it was supposed to be like, when a woman really cared and supported you.

Then one day, it happened. A moment he would never forget. The first time she touched him. Not the touch of a formal handshake, but the real thing. It was a Thursday, as their time had ended, when she opened the door to say goodbye and gave him that gentle touch on his arm. It was only for an instant, but it was the most important moment of his life.

She had reawakened something inside him. Something he had pushed deep down in his heart. But on that day, she brought it back out.

Of course, she acted like it never happened. She had to, obviously. She was married. But the signs were there if you looked hard enough. Her smile, how she faced him when he sat in her chair. The outfits she would wear for him. Roa had known other psychiatrists, but this was different, for both of them.

Then he blew it. She wasn't ready when he returned the affection. He should have known better. He should have waited. She clearly needed more time to dissolve her marriage, but he rushed it. God, he was so stupid.

It was when she stopped seeing him that he panicked. He had to explain. He had to make sure that she knew; that she knew he *understood*. He was foolish and had made things difficult for her. He had to make sure she knew that he would wait as long as it took. He wouldn't pressure her again. It could all go back to how it had been.

Then came the restraining order. It was more than unnecessary; it was devastating. He couldn't understand why she would do that. Why, after what they had together, would she want to hurt him? He couldn't call her; he couldn't see her. He was angry. Eventually it dawned on him. He remembered that he was sitting in his basement when he realized what happened. She hadn't given up on them. She probably didn't even want to issue the restraining order. It was her husband. Obviously, he had discovered something and become jealous. He realized Shannon had stronger feelings for another man and couldn't stand it. And he was a cop, so he would have no trouble getting a restraining order.

Roa had pieced it together. Her husband was afraid of losing Shannon, so he gave her an ultimatum. And what does a man use against a woman to make her stay? Her child.

There was only one flaw in her husband's plan. Roa was not going to let Shannon's husband do that to her. He and Shannon had a relationship that no one else did; it was a bond that no one else could even understand. He would not sit idly by and watch her be manipulated and controlled by a jealous husband, a piece-of-trash cop.

Roa paused when he noticed the note in his hands, glowing in the light from the fire. It had been pinned to the wall with all the pictures. It was *the* note. The one he used to get Ellie.

Written in Shannon's own hand, the small, yellow notepaper simply read, "Come to my office," and was signed "Dr. Mayer." She had once left it for him on the front door of her office suite when her receptionist was gone. Roa saved it, just as he saved everything else she'd given him.

Roa became committed to getting Ellie away from her manipulative father, and finally, after months of planning, he had done exactly that. He found out which police department Dennis Mayer worked for, then found the calendar for Ellie's school online. By studying the calendar and asking a few questions, he found the ideal day to get Ellie. It was one of the busiest days of the school year and one that also fell on the day Dennis Mayer normally picked her up from school.

Roa studied up on Mayer's top cases, and when it was time, he made an anonymous call with enough leading information to distract Mayer and his team. It bought Roa just enough time to find Ellie at school. Fortunately for him, she always waited for her parents around the corner from the main pickup area, where there was less of a traffic jam. Dressed in a suit, Roa got out of his car calmly, approached Ellie, and explained that her mother had sent him to pick her up. He showed her the note her mother had written. It was enough to get Ellie into his car. They were on the freeway before Ellie began to suspect something was wrong. By that point, it was too late.

He held the yellow note in his hand and felt it for the last time. That was eighteen months ago, an eternity to wait for Shannon. But he was patient. Love was worth waiting for. He had to allow time for the public to forget about Ellie before he could get her out of the country, to a place where Shannon could finally meet them. When they were safe, he planned to call her from a public phone in South America and let her know that they had made it. Then she could finally join them and have the kind of family she deserved, just the three of them.

Roa was elated; his hands began to shake. There had been so much to do. So much preparation, and now it was almost over. Everything was packed; everything was cleaned. In less than an hour they would head to the Los Angeles Airport and buy two one-way tickets to Miami.

Security for travelers in the United States had never been tighter, but there were still ways to get out unnoticed. Ellie had promised to cooperate for obvious reasons. So with new passports and a disguise they should have no problem getting to the East Coast. From there, they would leave through one of the last unsecured routes left: the Florida Keys.

A sailboat was reserved and waiting in Key West for a John Hernandez and his nine-year-old daughter, both citizens of Saint Kitts. They would sail due south and land in Havana, Cuba, by nightfall, where they would then board a plane and fly directly to Chile.

He thought again of Ellie and how she was finally opening up to him. She was so pretty and looked just like her mother. The same hair, the same eyes, even the same mannerisms. She looked so much like Shannon. So very, very much.

Roa tossed the note and the last of the pictures into the fire and watched them burn. It was a fitting end. In just a few days, the entire house would be bulldozed to the ground, and he and Ellie would be long gone.

—•—

It was the site of the first commercially successful oil well in the western United States, dubbed Number 4. The drill would eventually take its place in history, becoming the longest continually operating oil well in the world, not closing until over a hundred years later. In the 1870s, the sheer production from the drill spawned the birth of a nearby town called Mentryville, named after the well's original and extremely charismatic driller, Charles Alexander Mentry.

It was Mentry's original team that established the area, building houses along the ridge of the large canyon. One team member was Charleston Roa, an Irish immigrant who built a large house for his young bride; a house that would stay in the family for generations.

The dozens of old roads and trails running through the canyon also meant there were multiple ways out.

—•—

Sam Roa was still standing by the fireplace, watching the last of the embers die out, when he heard it. It was a sound he knew well.

Living alone on twenty acres of land held several very distinct advantages, one of which was the ability to hear cars coming up the long dirt road from very far away.

Roa turned toward the front window and, in a smooth motion, reached back to retrieve his gun from its holster. Then he turned off all the lights.

—•—

Shannon's BMW quietly rolled to a stop. She turned off both the engine and the headlights, staring at the silhouette of what appeared to be a large, old house. Everything suddenly became eerily quiet.

"Is this the house, Evan?" she asked in a low voice.

Evan sat up in the back seat and peered through the front window. "Yes."

Shannon could feel her anger quickly replaced by fear. She was so intent on getting here that she hadn't given much thought to what she would do when she arrived.

"I think Ellie was in the basement," Evan added.

Shannon looked out the driver's side window and could just make out the dark shapes of a small barn and a water tank. Closer to the house, she could clearly see a car parked beside the porch. It was facing them, but appeared empty. She took a deep breath and reached into her purse next to her, pulling out the small handgun she'd taken from her husband's collection. *God, where was Dennis?*

Shannon knew she should wait for the sheriffs, but had no idea when they would arrive, or if they would show up at all. The deputy who'd answered the phone there told Tania they would send someone out, but that was all she said. It could take a while, and the house already looked deserted. *What if he'd already left with Ellie?* Shannon wasn't about to keep waiting in her car knowing it could give Roa an even more significant head start.

Shannon nervously slid the gun into her coat pocket and took the keys out of the ignition so the car wouldn't make any sound when she opened the door.

She put her hand on the door handle before pausing to glance over her shoulder at the silhouettes of Evan and his mother. "Wait here. I'm gonna go have a look around."

In the dark, she couldn't see the worry on Evan's face. "I don't think you should do that," he whispered. "I think this man is dangerous."

The outline of Shannon's head didn't move. "I know that. But if he's already left with her, then every minute counts. I'll be careful. If I hear them inside I'll come back, and we'll wait for the sheriff."

"Do you promise?"

"I promise."

With that, Shannon quietly opened the door and eased her foot down onto the dead grass beneath the car. She stood up and gently closed the door, carefully pushing it shut with her hip. Only the faintest click could be heard. She scanned the area but couldn't see anything other than groups of trees and the road she'd come in on.

Shannon took her first step and cringed at the crunching sound the ground made under her shoe, even with the thin layer of grass on top. She moved more gingerly with her second step and managed to make significantly less noise.

Stopping several times to listen, she delicately tiptoed across the open area, heading for the left side of the house, where the car was parked. When she reached it, she stopped to listen again and then peered through the car's side windows. She couldn't make much out in the dark: several plastic bags and what looked like a larger duffle bag on the floorboard. Shannon stepped back and took in the whole car. It was a silver Honda Accord. What she didn't know was that that make and color was one of the most common cars in the United States.

Shannon looked over the roof of the car to the house. She couldn't see any lights or hear anything inside. Her heart began to sink. Were they already gone? Had she gotten there too late?

She continued moving past the car toward the back of the house. The area was unkempt, with old tools leaning against the side of the house and a lawn that was long gone. Hearing nothing, she approached the stairs to the raised back porch, gently placed her right foot on the first step, and cautiously applied pressure. It remained quiet. Gradually, she increased her weight until she was sure the board wouldn't give her away and then tried the next one. One step at a time, she made it to the top without any problems. But when she got close to the back door, one of the wooden planks let out a loud squeak. She froze. Not because of the squeak itself, but because the noise had come from a board behind her, not the one she was standing on.

—•—

In the car, Evan whispered nervously to his mother. "We have to do something."

Although obscured by the darkness, his mother shook her head. "No Evan, we don't. We need to wait until the police get here."

"And what if they don't? Or they take too long? What if the man is still here? Dr. Mayer is all by herself."

"Evan, we can't get help if we're all caught together." His mother reached into her purse and retrieved her phone. "We stay here. But if the police don't show up in ten minutes or we hear something, we call 911. Okay?"

Evan remained silent. She couldn't tell whether he agreed or not.

—•—

Shannon remained frozen. She could hear a heavy footstep behind her. She gasped and held her breath when a gun barrel was pressed into the small of her back.

A voice whispered in her ear. "How many?"

"Just me," she lied.

There was a long pause as Roa looked around the yard. "Turn around," he instructed.

Shannon turned slowly, almost shuffling, until she was looking directly into his dark eyes.

"Shannon!" Roa exclaimed. "What are you doing here?"

The sight of him made her stomach turn. She had once thought she would never have to see him again. "You know what I'm doing here," she sneered.

He was both surprised and excited to see her. It was not the reaction Shannon was expecting.

"You're here," he said. "You're finally here!"

"What?"

The glee was spreading across his face. "We've waited so long. I wasn't expecting to see you, at least not yet. My God, you're so beautiful!" His tone was becoming almost giddy, as he returned his gun to the holster at his back.

Shannon narrowed her eyes suspiciously. "What . . . are you talking about?"

"You knew," Roa smiled. "Didn't you? Of course you knew. I knew you would understand what all this was about. But I certainly didn't expect you to just *show up*," he added with a chuckle.

Shannon's mind was racing, but she tried to keep her attention on his words. She just wanted to know about Ellie, and to figure out how to get them both away from this lunatic alive. *Where was Ellie? Was she all right?* She just wanted her daughter, but her gut was warning her about Roa's ramblings. *He didn't seem nervous or afraid. He looked . . . elated. How could that be? How could he be elated if he just got found out?*

"I have everything together," he said excitedly. "The trip, the house, everything. *No one* is going to find us."

"Us?"

Roa nodded. "I have to admit, Ellie . . . had a little trouble for a while, but she's coming around now. She's talking, asking questions. She's even started calling me by name. Of course, once she sees you I'm sure she'll come out if it in no time." He took an excited breath and grabbed her arm with his large, rough hand. Shannon tensed.

"It's okay!" He smiled. "Don't worry, everything's fine. Everything's planned."

"Planned for what?"

"For *us*." He gave her a playful frown. "Don't tell me after all this time you didn't know what I was doing."

Shannon didn't answer. She was getting a very sick feeling.

"Look," he continued, "I know this is probably a little overwhelming, but don't worry. I've got everything worked out. Like I said, I wasn't expecting you, and honestly it was lucky you showed up when you did. I was—" Roa suddenly stopped, with his last words almost ringing in the air.

He remained still, staring at her, and slowly raised an eyebrow. He tilted his head slightly. "Wait a minute, how did you know I was leaving with Ellie tonight?"

Shannon's heart was still racing, beating faster each time he said Ellie's name. And while he talked, Shannon had been wondering how long it would take before he pondered that very question. Clearly there was something demented going on in his head, some kind of "plan." She didn't know what it was, but he'd referred to the three of them as "us" and was clearly excited she was there. Regardless of his intentions, Roa was now realizing that Shannon wasn't there for the reason he thought.

"I knew you understood why I took Ellie," he said. "That you knew what I was doing: removing her as leverage for your husband to use against you. Your silence over the last eighteen months *showed* me that you understood. That you believed in me. You knew it was a necessary evil, until we could be together." Roa's eyes now displayed a look of worry. "You knew all that, right?"

Again, Shannon didn't answer. Her mind was spinning, as she tried desperately to figure a way out of this that wouldn't get them killed.

"But if you knew that, and were waiting for me to contact you . . . why are you here, and how did you know tonight was the night?"

Shannon recognized she had to do something, and quickly. She cleared her throat and blurted out, "I couldn't wait."

Roa's eyes opened in surprise. As she saw him begin to process her answer, Shannon quickly reached out and put her hand on his arm.

The physical contact distracted him. He looked down and then back up at her with a swelling sense of joy. "I-I didn't . . . expect you." He smiled broadly. "But it doesn't matter. We can still go. We can all go together." He put his arm around her and turned them toward the old wooden door. "Come on, come on!" He opened the door and nudged her forward affectionately, stepping in behind her and turning on the inside light.

He watched as Shannon nervously scanned the room. It looked deserted. Only the small green table and chairs remained, pushed neatly into the corner. When her eyes circled back to him, he caught sight of her face in the light. "You look so beautiful, Shannon."

"Thank you," she said, playing along. Shannon quickly changed the subject. "Where's Ellie? I can't wait to see her."

Roa grinned. "And she can't wait to see you. Come with me." He walked past Shannon and led the way through the rest of the darkened house, turning on lights as they went. As he flipped on the living room light, Shannon noticed the plastic-covered furniture.

Suddenly Roa turned back around. "Wait! I just realized we need to rethink our story here. Your passport is under your real name."

"Oh, uh, right."

Roa thought to himself for a moment then held out his hand. "I have an idea. Let me see your passport for a minute."

Shannon's eyes widened with nervousness. "What?"

"Let me see your passport," he repeated. "I think I know how we can do this."

"I . . . uh." Shannon hesitated and took a small step back.

Roa rolled his eyes. "Shannon, just show me your passport. We don't have a lot of time."

She nodded and slowly reached into her coat pocket. She had no passport, and when he found that out he would know that she hadn't come there to join him at all.

Inside her pocket, she wrapped her hand around the grip of the gun, fumbling as she snaked her finger around the trigger. When she pulled it out, it would have to be fast. Her element of surprise would only buy her one or two seconds tops.

Ellie was in the house. And now a demented Roa was the only thing between them. She was running out of time. She had to do it. She had to do it right now! She took a quick, deep breath and then all at once yanked the gun out.

Unfortunately, the tip of the gun's hammer caught on the corner of her coat pocket.

28

Roa was a well-trained Marine, and he moved like one. When he saw the tip of the gun appear from her pocket, he moved like lightning and grabbed for the gun. It was pure instinct. Shannon's attempt at surprise had vanished. In an instant, he had her gun raised and pointed back at Shannon, even while his brain was still catching up with this sudden reversal. But once it did, his expression changed completely. His brief look of confusion very quickly turned to anger.

"Why did you do that, Shannon?" he said accusingly. "Tell me you weren't just trying to do what I think you were. Tell me that was an accident!" He kept the gun pointed at her, while the look of worry returned to his eyes. "Please tell me you're not one of them!"

"I—I—" she stuttered, raising both hands helplessly.

"Tell me!" Roa said, louder. He began shaking his head. "Tell me you didn't mean to do it. Tell me it was a coincidence that you showed up here tonight. That you're leaving with us." Roa began to glare intensely at her, growing angrier by the second. "Tell me, because I think you were going to shoot me with this gun. That you're here, not to join me, but to take Ellie back. To take her back to a life that I've spent almost two years trying to provide you a way out of!" Roa was shaking his head harder, and his hand holding the gun began to tremble. "Tell me you want to be with me and that I didn't just spend the last two years on a woman who's really one of *them*."

Shannon didn't move a muscle. She was petrified, staring at the gun just inches from her face. It was shaking erratically and Roa's finger was still on the trigger.

"Can you do that Shannon? Can you tell me *that*?"

She backed up and Roa smoothly stepped forward, following her.

"Why are you here, Shannon? Tell me. Tell me right now. Because if you're not with me now, after all this, then you were *never* with me! You just led me on and used me, like some kind of a lab rat." His face began to contort with anger, as he could see the truth emerge in Shannon's eyes. She wasn't there for him. She was there for her daughter, and only her daughter. He was nothing to her. No, he was worse, he was a criminal. In her eyes, he was just a criminal, a kidnapper, a *monster*. He dedicated two years of his life to her, and in just minutes, she had destroyed it. All of it. Every single thing he had cherished about her had deteriorated right before his eyes. In a single evening, the woman who he thought could save him had destroyed him instead.

"Sit down on that couch," Roa spat, motioning behind her.

Shannon backed up awkwardly while he followed. As she sat down on the plastic, Roa took a curious glance at Shannon's gun. He smirked, wondering if she realized that she'd brought a .22 pistol with her, one of the world's weakest calibers.

In that moment, while he was examining the gun, he saw a flash from the corner of his eye. From behind him, Evan swung the old rusty shovel as hard as he could, glancing off Roa's shoulder and into the side of his head, taking a large slice of skin with it.

Roa stumbled backward, stunned, and Evan quickly drew back and swung again. But Roa recovered quickly and this time stepped forward, closing the distance, and catching the shovel at the base of the handle. He twisted it easily out of Evan's hands, then stepped back and kicked the boy squarely in the chest. The impact sent Evan's weakened body into the hall, where he hit the wall and crumpled to the floor.

A piercing scream filled the room as Evan's mother charged with a can of pepper spray. Roa calmly ducked out of the way and blocked the stream of spray with the blade of his shovel. He then hit her with it in the same motion, knocking her down.

29

It was a busy night in Santa Clarita. Between the soft economy and improving weather, the number of burglaries and domestic disturbances was almost twice as high as last month. Deputy Bill Donaldson turned off the main road and drove up the dirt road toward Roa's house.

He rolled past, slowing to examine Shannon's BMW, and gradually pulled to a stop. After a few moments, he flipped on his searchlight and reached for the radio's microphone.

"Clarito, 130. At the house on Canyon Ridge for the possible two zero seven. Requesting 10-28 on California passenger plate 2DAS321."

A few moments later the dispatcher replied. "130, California 2DAS321 issued to Shannon Mayer of 785 Hilltop Drive, Glendale, on 2012 BMW, blue in color. No stolen."

He rotated the bright searchlight with his left hand, examining the barn and water tank, then the old Honda. Finally, he swept it across the house's lower level and then up across the top. The place looked very old. "Don't see anyone."

With that, Donaldson returned the mike to its holder and shifted the patrol car into park.

—•—

Evan's unconscious body fell hard against the floor next to Shannon, who was already bound and lying face down on the cold linoleum. The duct tape over her mouth prevented her from making any sound louder than a muted mumble. On her other side, Evan's mother was tied in the same position.

Roa straightened up, looking down at the three of them. *Sickening.* Without a word, he stepped over the trio and left the room.

Just before the door closed and plunged them into darkness, Shannon could see the blood leaking from around Evan's taped mouth and dripping onto the floor.

—•—

Roa was returning from the far end of the hallway, thinking how best to dispose of the bodies, when he heard a loud knocking on the front door. He jumped back and ducked into the bathroom, waiting a moment before tilting his head back out past the doorframe. The front of the house was now awash in bright light. Roa cursed under his breath and turned to look in the mirror. The large bandage along the side of his jaw was more than a tad obvious. He needed to think. The loud knocking came again, but this time, he thought, it sounded like pounding.

In front of the house and getting no reply, Deputy Donaldson took a few steps over and looked through the large living room window. He could see the place was sparsely decorated and looked like someone might have just moved in. He was about to return to knock on the door again when he saw movement inside. A large man had emerged from the hallway and was walking toward him.

When the door opened, Donaldson was greeted by a man in his late forties, bald, and just a few inches taller than himself.

"What's going on?" the man asked, squinting into the bright lights of the patrol car.

"Are you Sam Roa?" the deputy asked.

"Yeah. Who are you? What's going on?"

"Sheriff's Department," Donaldson replied, peering inside over Roa's shoulder. "We received a call a little while ago indicating there might be a problem out here."

Roa feigned a confused look. "What kind of problem?"

Donaldson examined Roa's face and bandage. "I'm not really sure. What happened to your face there?"

"I was just trimming some trees," he lied. "One of the damn limbs snapped back and took a piece out of my jaw. Guess it didn't like being chopped down."

Roa was trying to keep the deputy calm. If the man sensed any danger, this was about to become much harder. Roa just needed an opportunity.

Deputy Donaldson frowned and peered inside again. "I see. Is that your BMW out there?"

Roa looked out, squinting again into the light. "I only see your car."

The turn was only momentary, but it was all Roa needed. As Donaldson turned to motion over his shoulder at Shannon's BMW, Roa was on him instantly. He moved hard and fast, hitting Donaldson under his jaw and pushing his hand up and over, following the officer's face. At the same time, Roa wrapped his leg around Donaldson's closest ankle, which kept him from stepping back to balance. Donaldson toppled over backward, with Roa almost riding him down onto the wooden porch.

By the time they hit the floor, the officer already had his gun out, but Roa quickly knocked it away. He reached behind his back, where he'd stashed Shannon's gun, and drew it out of his belt in less than a second.

—•—

Shannon heard the sickening popping sound coming from the front of the house. She closed her eyes and laid her face on the floor, her crying muffled through the duct tape. She knew the pounding on the front door was the sheriff's department, and she hoped beyond hope that if those were gunshots, it was the officer shooting.

After a long silence she heard something scraping in the hall, a grating against the floor. Whatever it was, it was coming their way.

Less than thirty seconds later, the door to her room burst open again. Shannon struggled to look up and saw the silhouette of Roa's figure stumble in. He was dragging something. When Shannon saw what it was, she almost threw up. He was dragging the officer's dead body.

Roa pulled Donaldson's corpse to the other side of the room and, with some effort, set him upright and slouching against the wall. He reached forward and removed the officer's radio before finally standing up and taking a deep breath. This was a problem, a big problem.

Above all, Marines were trained to adapt to a changing environment. Roa's mind was racing, trying to adjust his plan to fit a situation that was becoming more complicated by the minute. Making the women and the boy disappear was one thing, but making a cop disappear was a much harder task. They knew where he was, and soon, when he didn't reply, they would send backup—if they hadn't already. He now had very little time.

He stared down at the deputy's body. Having taken the .22 from Shannon, he used it to kill the deputy. After falling on top of the officer, he shoved the gun over the lip of the man's bulletproof vest and unloaded the entire magazine straight down into his chest. The .22 caliber rounds were small enough that Roa was able to keep them all inside the body, without exiting, which meant no blood spatter. There was no way to clean up blood spatter in the mere minutes he had left to escape.

He turned and looked downward at Shannon, who was still lying face down. He couldn't believe it. He just couldn't believe she had turned on him. But now he was in a survival situation. He had to cut loose his feelings for her and focus. There was still one comforting thought. Ellie was just like her mother, but she hadn't been poisoned. And now he was developing a real relationship with her. Shannon betrayed him, but he still had Ellie.

With a growing distaste to even look at Shannon, he reached down and did one last thing. He used his shirt to wipe the prints from her gun, then reached down and placed the tiny semi-automatic back in her hand to add her prints again. He released her wrist and watched as she threw the gun away in protest.

Roa shrugged. It didn't matter. It wouldn't fool anyone, nor would the lack of blood spatter, but together they would create some initial confusion and slow the investigation down. At least in the beginning, which is all he really needed. He'd be at the airport in less than an hour and in the air shortly after that on the first flight he could get. The police would spend at least that much time trying to figure out what happened and where to set up their checkpoints. Hell, it would take them far longer just to find the car, and when they did, they would still be looking for Samuel Roa, not his new identity.

Roa was interrupted by the squawk of the radio still in his hands. The dispatcher announced the deputy's backup would arrive in ten minutes. He knew it would be closer to six once they realized the deputy was not answering his radio. Even six minutes was more than enough time to disappear into the canyon. But he had to leave now.

—•—

Young Ellie Mayer looked up as the basement lights came back on. She had been sitting silently in the dark, wrapped in a blanket, wondering what was causing all the commotion. Now she heard the pounding down the stairs. He was coming, and fast.

Ellie slipped her small necklace and locket inside the arch of her shoe. It was the only thing she still had to remember her mother by, and she'd managed to keep it hidden from him all this time. She didn't want to leave it behind.

They were about to leave. She had been lonely for so long, constantly crying herself to sleep. But finally, the man named Sam told her about the trip, which gave her something to look forward to. He also began removing things from her room. She was going to see her mother for the first time since he'd taken her. He told her he felt bad and wanted to give her back to her parents. If she was good, they would go on a long trip to a place where he would give Ellie back. And that day had finally arrived.

She grabbed her bag of clothing and stood up in anticipation, tucking a lock of hair behind her ear. Nothing, not even whatever was happening upstairs, could keep her from wanting to leave.

The door unlocked quickly from the other side and opened to a disheveled Roa wearing a look of urgency. "We're leaving," he blurted, and grabbed her wrist. He quickly climbed the stairs with Ellie trailing closely behind him, clutched in his iron grip. Her soft bag bounced around her knees as Ellie almost had to hop from stair to stair to keep up. When they reached the top, Roa pushed the door open and pulled Ellie into the hallway. "Shh," he sounded, and put a finger over his lips, now whispering. "We have to get to the car as soon as we can."

Ellie nodded quietly. She was eager and more than ready.

—•—

Shannon remained face down in pitch-blackness. She couldn't see anything at all and was beginning to lose her orientation. She had struggled so much on the floor that she couldn't remember whether Evan, or his mother, lay to her right or left side. Shannon stopped moving. She was having trouble breathing through just her nose and was at risk of suffocating.

At that moment, as she lay helplessly on the cold floor, neither she nor Ellie knew that through the wall, they were less than ten feet from each other. It was the nearest the two had been in a year and a half.

—•—

Ellie followed Roa in silence, as she had been commanded, away from her mother, down the hallway, and toward the front of the house. Roa was still holding her tightly by the wrist.

When he finally reaching the living room, Roa jumped back, as the front door was violently kicked open from the outside. A large figure stepped out of the blinding light and into the house.

Ellie screamed. She recognized that shape; it was her father.

30

Roa was stunned, but he managed to keep Ellie behind him. His gun was instantly out of its holster.

Dennis Mayer stood in the doorway, his rigid features bathed in the spotlight emanating from the patrol car outside. In his right hand, Roa could see the shadow of a gun. Mayer's eyes softened momentarily when he saw Ellie, then hardened again as he glared at Roa with immense anger.

Roa did not lose his cool. He whirled Ellie around him, placing her between Mayer and himself. Roa's thoughts were racing as fast as ever. He had very little time, and now, after seeing her father, it would be nearly impossible to get Ellie into the car with any level of cooperation. He would have to force her in and try to explain things later.

And as much as he disliked the man, Roa didn't want to kill yet another person. It would only make things harder for him. But it was clear from the look on Mayer's face that they were going to have to go *through* him to get out. This was going to have to happen fast.

Dennis Mayer's eyes dropped again to his daughter, standing in front of Roa. He could not imagine what she had gone through, or what mental state she was in. Was she brainwashed or did she still remember? Mayer stared at his daughter, now wondering only one thing. *Did she remember what he had practiced with her so many times in the past? Did she remember what to do when he gave her the signal?*

He prayed she remembered the most important thing he had ever taught her: when to drop to the ground.

—•—

Shannon lifted her head when she heard yelling in the hallway followed by two thundering gunshots. A chunk of drywall fell to the floor as one of the bullets passed through the wall over her head. What she heard next nearly stopped Shannon's heart: her daughter's screams.

From the far end of the hall, Shannon could hear heavy steps coming her way again. This time they were mixed with the sound of Ellie wailing. She lowered her head to the floor, beyond devastated. She had come all this way only to find herself utterly helpless in the end and unable to save her daughter, who was now almost within reach.

The steps grew louder, as did her daughter's crying. There was a long, foreboding pause in the hallway before the door to Shannon's room was pushed opened.

The door seemed to open in slow motion. Now in the light and looking up from the floor with blurred vision, Shannon saw the large silhouette in the doorway. It was an odd shape and appeared to slowly bend down and separate into two. Before she could understand what was happening, one of the shapes fell to Shannon's side on the floor. Two small arms wrapped themselves around her bound body and sobbed. It was Ellie. The silhouette was Ellie!

The second shape approached and knelt down beside her. As he bent down, Shannon recognized the unmistakable form of her husband.

The tape was painfully pulled from her mouth, and Shannon gasped. "Ellie! My Ellie!" She closed her eyes as Ellie kissed her all over her face. She quickly opened them again and barked to her husband. "Check Evan!"

It was all she got out before her words dissolved into a blubbering mess.

None of them heard the faint sound of a siren in the distance.

EPILOGUE

The temperature had dropped slightly as the last of the season's cold winds battled the warm springtime sun through a thinly overcast sky. Across the valley, a cool breeze from the Santa Anas began to pick up as the afternoon made its way into evening.

At the top of the large stone steps, Evan sat quietly with his backpack, watching dozens of other teenagers mill around, waiting for their rides. Most were standing in small groups, talking and laughing.

Two seniors headed down the steps of the high school's main entrance. As they passed him, one of the boys kicked Evan's backpack, sending it tumbling.

"Whoops, sorry," he said, laughing.

The second teen looked back at Evan and laughed just as hard. "What a dork."

The first boy, a tall red-haired kid, stopped. "Watch this." He hopped a couple steps back up toward Evan and abruptly made a motion as if he was going to hit him. The boy was expecting Evan to flinch, but he didn't. Instead, he jumped to his feet with clenched fists.

The antagonist looked at Evan with a hint of nervousness. Then he turned and leapt back down to where his friend was standing. "He's such a freak."

Evan silently leaned down and reached for his backpack, pulling it back up onto the top step.

"Hey there!" It was a female voice.

Evan looked to his right and was surprised to see Tania Cooper standing several feet away. Her short brown hair fell in perfect symmetry along her cheekbones, complementing her light skin and hazel eyes. She smiled broadly at Evan. "Need a ride?"

"Hi," Evan said, noticing the nearby boys staring at her. "I didn't know you were coming."

She shrugged. "I asked Dr. Mayer if I could pick you up."

"Oh, okay, thanks." Evan stood up and slung the pack over his shoulder. He trotted down the stairs to where she was standing. "Where are you parked?"

"Over there." Tania nodded toward the street. She observed even more teens staring at her and Evan. Some had their mouths open. She continued to watch the gawkers in amusement as she and Evan walked across the grass, headed for her car. Tania hid her grin, and deliberately slid her hand around the inside of Evan's arm.

He looked down at her hand, and then at her.

Tania winked. "Keep walking." As they neared her small Toyota, she leaned in close. "Do you know how to drive?"

"Yes."

"Good, here." She handed Evan her keys. "You drive."

"Really?"

"Yes. And make sure you open my door for me."

Evan did as instructed. He opened the passenger door and watched Tania slide in gracefully, and with a loud giggle. After she tucked her dress in, he closed the door, and walked around the front to the driver's side. Before he got in, Evan glanced back toward the school. *Everyone* was now watching them.

He slid into the driver's seat and closed the door, turning to smile at Tania. "Thanks for that."

She winked again. "That was fun."

He pulled the seatbelt across his chest and started the car. After a few more checks to his side mirror than were necessary, he pulled out into the lane.

"So how are you?" Tania asked.

"Not bad." He lied. He almost told her the truth but changed his mind. There was no point. She couldn't do anything but feel sorry for him, so why bother. When he began taking the Valium a few days before, it had given him some temporary relief, but he was beginning to have problems again. Something felt like it was burning inside his chest. He was going to talk to Dr. Mayer about it.

Evan turned left onto Broadway and headed for Glendale Avenue. "This is a nice car."

"Thanks, I'll tell the bank you said that."

Evan laughed.

"So, are you looking forward to school being over?"

"I've been looking forward to it being over for about three years."

This time Tania laughed. "I hated high school. I don't know what it was, but when I became a junior it just felt like everyone was acting really stupid."

"I know what you mean. Did you go to college?"

"No." She shrugged. "College is expensive. My parents don't have much money, and I didn't want to go into debt up to my eyeballs. So I decided to learn some actual skills instead."

"That's pretty much where I am. It's nice to know I'm not alone."

Tania nodded and watched as they passed a group of female high school runners. "So . . . how are you?"

"Uh, didn't you already ask me that?"

"No, I mean *really*, as in after the whole Ellie thing."

"Oh that. I'm okay. I have some bumps and bruises, but I'll be fine." He turned to her as they stopped for a traffic light. "How is Ellie, anyway?"

Tania shrugged. "They're not really sure yet. They have to do more tests. But right now, Dr. Mayer and her husband aren't letting Ellie out of their sight."

"I can understand that."

Tania became quiet for a moment. Then she looked straight at Evan. "You know you're a hero, right?"

He chuckled. "I don't know about that. I helped, but that's about it." He looked at Tania, who was giving him a very sarcastic frown. "Well, I guess I did figure out where Ellie was."

"Evan," she began, with a touch of sarcasm. "You did a lot more than that. I was there for some of it, remember? And Dr. Mayer told me what happened at that house. You saved Ellie. You're a hero."

"I mostly just got beat up."

Tania shook her head. "There's more to courage than winning, Evan." She was quiet for a minute. "You know, I had a boyfriend. He was a jerk. I broke up with him because I believe we all deserve to live happily ever after."

"Yeah?"

"Yeah," she replied. "And with him, there wouldn't have been a happily ever after."

As he drove, he could see from the corner of his eye that she was still watching him.

"Honestly, I don't know if Ellie will have a happily ever after," she said. "But you gave her a chance. Thanks to you, Evan, she at least gets an *ever after*, which is a lot better than the alternative."

Evan pulled into the small parking lot and parked, a little crooked, in a corner spot. He and Tania got out and climbed the back stairs up to the offices. When they reached Dr. Mayer's door, Evan held it open for Tania and followed her in.

Reception was empty. Dr. Mayer had cancelled all of her appointments for two weeks. In fact, that day was the only day she'd come into the office at all.

Evan thanked Tania again for the ride as she sat down at her desk, and he continued down the hallway toward Dr. Mayer's office. When he reached it, he knocked lightly on the wide door and waited.

—•—

Inside, Shannon sat at her desk next to her daughter, who was drawing on a large piece of paper. It was part of the play therapy, and just the beginning of a long road ahead for them both. Drawing pictures was a common technique used to help victims externalize damaging experiences, to bring them out where they could be dealt with.

Shannon heard the knock, and gently placed her hand on Ellie's back as she stood up. She crossed the room and quietly opened the door.

"Hello, Evan."

"Hi," he said, and stepped into the room. He spotted Ellie at the large desk with the paper in front of her.

"Ellie, honey, look who's here. It's Evan."

Ellie wore a beautiful white dress with blue and green flowers, and her hair was pulled back into a ponytail. She stopped and looked up at Evan. Without a word, Ellie stood up and walked around the desk. She went to Evan and wrapped her little arms around his waist.

He bent over and hugged her back. "Hi Ellie, how are you?"

"Good."

Dr. Mayer watched the tender moment and placed her hand over her mouth. She blinked the tears away and dropped her hand onto Evan's shoulder. "Come in, Evan."

He nodded and moved away from the door. He crossed the carpeted floor and leaned against the familiar leather chair.

They both watched Ellie return to the desk and sit back down. "How are things?"

"Pretty good," he replied, with an optimistic tone. "My mom got a new job."

"Is that right?"

"Yeah. A customer in her restaurant told her he'd been watching her and wanted to hire her to manage the wait staff at his own restaurant. Some fancy place in Montrose. So we're going to go looking for a new apartment."

"That's great, Evan."

"And get this, this man Mr. Friedricks also said he has an older car he's selling and asked if I wanted to buy it. He said I could work part-time at his restaurant to pay it off."

"Incredible." Shannon smiled, and maintained an innocent expression. She was happy to see Evan excited, even for the moment. He had done so much for her, things for which she could never repay him. But it didn't mean she couldn't try. Of course, it would be a breach of ethics to compensate him directly. She could, however, make a few phone calls.

"And how are you feeling?" she asked.

"Better. Still healing though."

"That's not what I meant."

"Oh." He glanced again at Ellie, her head down and the pen working away in her hand. "The Valium helps, but it feels like it's wearing off. I've been waking up with a lot of pain in my chest."

Shannon's expression grew serious. "Evan, I think we need to stop with the Valium."

"Why?"

Before she could answer, there was another knock on her door. "Come in," Shannon said.

Tania opened the door and looked at them both. "She's here," she said quietly.

Shannon approached the door just as her sister entered. Mary looked tired, but her eyes searched the room intently until she found Ellie. When she did, she began to cry, and held her arms out. Mary dropped to her knees as Ellie abandoned the paper again and ran to her, throwing herself into her aunt's arms.

Mary cried hard, stroking Ellie's soft hair. "Thank God," she whispered. "Thank God."

As Evan watched the two, a tall, older man discreetly stepped into the room behind Mary. His hair was thick and gray, and he was dressed in an old flannel shirt and jeans.

Mary cleared her throat and looked up. "Sis, allow me to introduce Daniel Taylor."

Shannon extended her hand. "It's nice to meet you, Mr. Taylor. I hear you were a hard man to find."

Taylor shook her hand. "Not for your sister, apparently."

The large man smiled at Ellie from under his thick brows. Next he turned his piercing eyes to look at Evan. "So this is him," Taylor said. "You're the one who can see things, are you?"

Evan didn't say anything. He took a nervous step back, and glanced at Dr. Mayer.

Taylor followed, stepping closer toward him. He towered over Evan and looked him up and down, examining him.

Evan tried to back up farther but ran into the arm of the chair.

A devilish grin slowly spread across Taylor's face. "Relax boy. I'm not here to hurt you. I'm here to keep it from killing you . . ."

AFTERWORD

Anne Keyes stared at her living room with a mingled sense of hope and dread. It was eerily quiet as the morning sun began to rise, shining through her front window. Over the next few hours, it would begin its work, thawing the winter morning frost and warming the air to an almost balmy fifty degrees.

Keyes glanced down at her watch again. It was 6:50 a.m. People would be arriving shortly. She was hoping for fifty this time, but worried it would be far less. The numbers had dwindled rapidly over the last month. She couldn't blame them, at least not out loud. In her own mind, she herself battled between feelings of appreciation and disgust. Appreciation for those still dedicated to sticking it out, and a secret though guilty feeling of disgust for the majority who didn't. *Who cared about the holidays?*

The large wooden table behind her was covered with flyers. A smaller table against the wall supported several large canisters of hot coffee and stacks of paper cups. Next to the cups were four dozen doughnuts in pink boxes.

She hoped to be on the road by 8 a.m. sharp.

———

Twelve people. *Twelve lousy people.* That was all that showed up. Her sense of despair deepened as the hour approached eight o'clock. She knew from experience that most of those who were coming had already arrived. There wouldn't be many stragglers. It meant they would be lucky to cover a third of the distance she had mapped out. She forced herself to ignore the frustration and remember that thirteen was better than one.

She watched silently as the group members chatted with each other, coffee cups in their hands. She was suddenly overcome by a feeling of loneliness as she thought about her life now and everything she had to do, alone. The doorbell rang, and she shook herself out of it. *Fourteen is better than thirteen,* she mused.

Crossing the carpeted floor, she opened the white front door to find two people standing on her porch. She didn't recognize either of them.

"Good morning," she said, with a feigned smile.

The larger of the two nodded. "Good morning. Are you Anne Keyes?" He already knew the answer.

"Yes, I am. Are you here to help?"

The dark-haired man raised an eyebrow, and peered over her shoulder at the volunteers in her living room. "Are we interrupting?"

Anne looked at him curiously. "You're not here for the search?"

"No, ma'am."

"Oh," she frowned. "What can I do for you then?"

"My name is Dennis Mayer, from the LAPD. We'd like to talk to you about your case."

Anne's heart jumped. "Los Angeles Police? Did you find—"

Dennis raised his hand cautiously, cutting her off. "No, ma'am. I'm sorry, I didn't mean to imply that." He looked over her shoulder again at the assembled group inside. "Would you mind if we talked privately?"

—•—

Anne asked one of her volunteers to go through the details of the search, while she led her visitors to the small dining room on the other side of the kitchen.

"We're sorry. We can see you're busy," began Dennis. "But we wanted to talk to you about your daughter's case."

"Of course." She nodded, looking back and forth between the two visitors. "You just caught me a little off guard. I didn't know LA was working on the case too."

"They're not officially," replied Dennis. "I'm retired. I'm more of a private investigator now, following a handful of special cases. Yours being one of them."

"I see," Anne replied. "Well, I'm more than happy to answer any questions you have. I can use all the help I can get."

Dennis could hear the people in the other room, and glanced around the corner before he continued. When he did, he spoke in a lowered tone. "We're familiar with most of the details regarding your daughter Katie. But there were a couple questions we wanted to ask you, things that generally take a while to be updated in the case file. First and foremost, has anyone been in contact with you? For example, a ransom note, a phone call, anything at all. It could even be something that struck you as odd, but you assumed to be completely unrelated. Even a strange comment from a friend."

Anne pondered the question. "No, nothing overt. And I'm trying to think of anything *odd*, but nothing comes to mind. To be honest," she said, with a longing look, "when you can't sleep for four months, your mind tries to connect anything and everything."

The truth was that Anne Keyes didn't know what to think. There were so many things about her daughter's disappearance that she couldn't understand. How could she just disappear less than eight blocks from her own house on a neighborhood sidewalk? How could it be that no one had seen anything? Christ, most everyone on the block knew each other; if not by first name, then certainly by last.

They lived in a nice area, and Katie was twelve years old. She rarely walked home by herself, and even when she did, she knew what to do if approached by a stranger. The police thought that might mean Katie had been abducted by someone she knew. But they'd checked everyone—family, friends . . . They'd even traced every person who had ever called or texted her phone.

Anne shook her head, still thinking about the question. "I'm sorry, I can't think of a single thing."

"I understand." Dennis nodded sympathetically. "Just one last question. Do you know for how many of those contacts, the people who called or texted your daughter's phone, did the police conduct a full background search?"

"I'm not sure. Most of them I think."

"I see," answered Dennis. He thought again about the group in her living room. He had counted twelve when they walked through. Anne's numbers were falling fast. It was normal after a few months of searching. Most volunteers eventually got pulled away, having to attend to their own lives. It was understandable, but it left the victim's family in an increasingly large emotional vacuum, lost in a void of loneliness and despair. She did still have these twelve, he thought, and probably several more who couldn't make it that day. But it didn't help that the mood was not an optimistic one.

Dennis could see the disappointment filling Anne Keyes's eyes as she realized her two visitors didn't know any more than she did. He finally bobbed his head slightly, turning and looking down past his right shoulder.

Evan was facing away from him, examining several photographs on a nearby shelf. His gaze finally circled back, and he looked up to Dennis Mayer. Evan then turned to Anne and spoke quietly, for the first time. "Can we see her bedroom?"

ACKNOWLEDGEMENTS

Special thanks to Autumn, Julie, Liz, Susan, Don, Tony, Dennis, and Karen, for their expert advice and proofing help. I have learned (the hard way) that mistakes in books can be harder to find than needles in haystacks.

ABOUT THE AUTHOR

 Michael C. Grumley lives in Northern California with his wife and two young daughters where he works in information technology. He's an avid reader, runner, and, most of all, a devoted father. He is the author of three previous thrillers, *Breakthrough*, *Amidst the Shadows*, and *LEAP*.